About the author

Pieter Woittiez was born some time ago in The Netherlands. While his work was science based, in the field of biological and medical sciences, in his spare time he discovered a creative streak. In his younger years he used this talent to imaginatively renovate old homes. Later, his creativity led to pursuits such as lead-glassing, ceramics (sculptural works), drawing, painting, screen-printing, and of course writing. *The Chosen One* is one of his many stories and is the first published. Pieter is recently widowed from his wife Nel and has one daughter. He is proudly Australian, migrating in the late 1950s, and has lived in Sydney, Newcastle, and now Canberra. His interests include politics, gardening, the arts, travel and board games. He believes life is mysterious and interesting, but far too short.

This is a work of fiction. Names, characters, businesses, places, events and incidents are either the products of the author's imagination or used in a fictitious manner. Any resemblance to actual persons, living or dead, or actual events is purely coincidental.

The Chosen One

Pieter Woittiez

The Chosen One

Vanguard Press

VANGUARD PAPERBACK

© Copyright 2023
Pieter Woittiez

The right of Pieter Woittiez to be identified as author of
this work has been asserted by him in accordance with the
Copyright, Designs and Patents Act 1988.

All Rights Reserved

No reproduction, copy or transmission of this publication
may be made without written permission.
No paragraph of this publication may be reproduced,
copied or transmitted save with the written permission of the
publisher, or in accordance with the provisions
of the Copyright Act 1956 (as amended).

Any person who commits any unauthorised act in relation to
this publication may be liable to criminal
prosecution and civil claims for damages.

A CIP catalogue record for this title is
available from the British Library.

ISBN 978-1-80016-526-7

Vanguard Press is an imprint of
Pegasus Elliot Mackenzie Publishers Ltd.
www.pegasuspublishers.com

First Published in 2023

Vanguard Press
Sheraton House Castle Park
Cambridge England

Printed & Bound in Great Britain

Dedication

I dedicate this story to my late wife, Nelly. You encouraged and motivated me to adventures I otherwise would have missed out on, and even now your ashes make my grevillea flower. Thank you Nel. Much love Pieter.

Acknowledgements

Thanks to my always busy daughter, Helen, for having spent so much time proofreading, advising and making the presentation suitable and attractive to submit for publication.

THE CHARACTERS

Marquita	The heroine of the story
Janitis	Marquita's close friend and beloved
Jacquito	Janitis's father
Estabella	The girl that got away and established a new empire
Breer	Marquita's brother
Baruta	Marquita's father
Mariotte	Marquita's mother
Sniffer	Janitis's horse
Fearless	A horse
Marmillo	Westland friend
Warda	Marmillo's sister
Wobbles	Marmillo's brother
Sherba	Maid at Baruta's house
Tintilla	Sherba's eight-year-old daughter
Jansino	Servant at Baruta's house
Wally	A guard at Super Castle
Marculas	Commander in charge of the guards
Calli & Collo	Twin brothers
Shalina	A yakapacca
Brot	Shalina's son
Ariotto	Companion at Super Castle
Jambuloo	Parents' choice for Marquita's partner
Sjasta	Estabella's assistant

1
Baruta

It was more than just the shine of satisfaction. Utter happiness radiated from Baruta's forceful face. It had been a long time to come to this, many decades; it was the crown on his achievements, the ultimate accolade of his life's work. He had achieved much; it had not just been thrown into his lap, it had been the result of hard work, persistence and above all devotion to the beliefs and principles of the Word, the sacred text recorded on stone tablets only the learned could decipher and interpret.

Marquita, their Marquita, his Marquita, his beautiful daughter, the apple of his eye, she had been chosen, she was the Chosen One this biennium, picked out by the Inner Six and approved by the Upper Host to be the virgin bride this spring, with the change of the season on Great Renewal Day.

What honour! Honour for her, honour because of her superb qualities, her beauty and her bearing, her poise, her devotion and most of all her purity and intelligence. And what honour to his family. This would place them on a new level from upper middle-class respectability to a level where they would now be among the very high stratum of the community and have access to all those at the highest level. He was already well advanced in the local hierarchy by being on the senior advisory board that deliberated on community matters and reported their findings to the Inner Six. As such he had already an elevated level of respect and favour in the community. This was a considerable achievement, particularly for someone of his background. His parents had just been unremarkable, ordinary folks, but he always, from a very young age, had stood out, for trying to do the right thing, whenever, wherever; being precise and excellent in his actions and unobtrusive at the same time. But most of all for his devotion. His devotion and adherence to the principles of the Dogma, laid down in the Sacred Text, the Word, interpreted by the wise ones over many, very many years and enforced and protected by the Inner Six and personified in the Upper Host.

It was so unusual for someone of his background to rise to the level that he had. Prejudices and ties between families in society made it almost impossible for someone, anyone, to climb up the ladder and be elevated to achieve a higher rank in society, but he had done it, he had managed what most would think the impossible. Step by step in his quiet unobtrusive way. And because of the way he behaved and acted, no one ever seemed to have taken exception to his rise or made disparaging remarks about his unremarkable background.

But now it was the biggest step up he would be taking, in his Marquita being the Chosen One for the new season. It also meant that if one of the old ones from the Inner Six passed away, he would now be a possible candidate to fill such an extraordinary position.

2
Marquita

Marquita was puzzled and confused. It all had happened so suddenly. When after some pain in her lower belly she had started to bleed, she had not panicked. Her parents were not secretive, certainly not about sexual matters, and her mum had long before explained to her in detail what would happen to her in future and that this was not a matter to be feared, but an occasion for celebration as it meant a transition to a new phase in life. A change from girlhood into womanhood, the passing of a border; a new path would open up in front of her, a more mature path: the entry into the life of the grown-ups.

But all the same, Marquita's immediate reaction had been one of dread, disappointment, even panic. Janitis had been her first thought; Janitis, her only close friend and playmate. She no longer would be allowed even to talk to him. The rules were strict, and there were no exemptions. When a girl entered this stage of life, she no longer was allowed male company, except for close family. Not until she was married would she be able to talk with any boy, and even after marriage her contact with men other than her husband and family would be restricted. Such were the rules and they were strictly adhered to. She had not even been able to say farewell to Janitis; her requests to do so were strongly, even fiercely denied. It did not amaze her. She had known for a very long time what would happen when she passed this border. But now she was grieving.

The grieving had started immediately, it burnt in her fiercely. "Janitis, Janitis," she kept saying silently over and over again, reaching out to him with her thoughts, concentrating all her mental efforts in trying to make him hear her messages and hoping to hear an answer. But nothing came, and she slumped over in bleak despair. Mariotte, her much loved 'Marty-Mum' and the servants had tried to cheer her up, bringing her presents and congratulating her on her entry into womanhood, but they had left discouraged by her lack of response. She who had always been so gay and outgoing, such a fun girl, seemed to have fallen into a dark place of despondency.

But then after a few days Marquita started to think about the promises Janitis and she had made to each other, the promises of belonging to each other for life, the agreement that when she was 'brought out' and presented as a woman ready for marriage, Janitis would propose and ask her father for her hand in marriage.

This prospect was of great worry to Janitis, as girls usually married a man older than themselves and of an equal or superior status in society. The thought of approaching her father, a man of influence and distinction, while he was only a mere boy and of insignificant background, was of great concern to him.

Marquita sighed. She missed the outdoors. On rainy and dark days, it could be nice and cosy inside, but as soon as the sun was out, she liked to roam outside, wander away from home, discover what was out there, beyond where there were no houses, beyond the borders of the township, walking, searching, discovering. Same as Janitis, that was what he too liked to do more than anything else. It was thus that their friendship had grown and developed. Any new plant, insect, any animal they saw was straight away pointed out to the other and so over time they developed a good knowledge of their environment.

The landscape too they had studied while they walked long and far. Both Janitis and she were told by their parents never to go into the swamp, not to go near it, but Janitis had found a ridge of elevated ground, leading to what looked like an island in the swamp, but was in actual fact a peninsula that could be reached by way of the curved ridge connecting to an oval raised area right in the middle of the swamp. He had taken her there and the quietness and freshness made her sigh a sigh of delight, she could not think of anything more beautiful.

"When we get married, that's where I want to live," she had said to Janitis.

But he had just smiled and looked wistfully at the range beyond the swamp. "One day we will go and look what's beyond there. This is great but there may be better country to grow things."

It was not possible to do that in a day and be back for the evening meal in time, so it could not happen now. As far as they knew nobody had ever been beyond the ridge, and few people would do what they just had done, as fear of the swamp was universal. But Janitis and Marquita were different, and they knew it, and kept most of their adventures a secret from their parents. *One day after we are married, we will go and see what lies beyond the ridge*, of that, she was sure.

In the meantime, she just needed to make the best of her confinement to the house, for she would not be allowed outside unchaperoned and that meant she would be unable to enjoy her usual outdoor activities.

Both Sherba, the house help, and Tintilla, her eight-year-old daughter, called in regularly, trying to entertain her. Marquita had to get used to the way they treated her now, no longer as a child, but as a grown up. Flattered on the one hand, she felt somewhat uncomfortable, as if she had changed personalities. It was altogether a bit hard to take, losing her freedom to be able to go where she wanted to go, losing her adventures with Janitis which had been daily events and being confined to this room till Mum would decide for her to go out. But then it would be chaperoned and limited to occasions of her mother's choice.

This had been minor compared to what happened next. Once every two years, six weeks before the consummation of 'the perfect marriage', which was the marriage between the Chosen One and the Upper Host, the novices were introduced to society. It was an exciting event for all the new young women. Their beauty was paraded for the community, all dressed up to the nines, of course, all looking their best. Parents behind the scenes had already for some time been busy to match the girls with suitable future husbands.

After the girls had been paraded through the big hall, musicians would strike up a tune for the dance. All eyes were trained on the young ladies, to see who each would lead off with. Although not a firm rule, it was more or less expected that the boy being accepted for the first dance, would most likely be her future husband.

Baruta and her mum had been busy looking for the most suitable match for Marquita, but when Baruta told Marquita that Jambuloo was their choice for the first dance, Marquita had shaken her head decidedly.

"No, Dad, no way. Janitis gets the first dance and then he will ask you for approval to marry me soon after."

Baruta had burst out laughing. "Janitis, nice boy, but your child days are over. Now it is time to get serious about your future life. If Jambuloo is objectionable to you, there are two other possibilities, both acceptable to Mum and me, but forget about Janitis."

What happened next struck Baruta like a slap in his face. His always obedient and placid daughter, shook her head. "No, Dad, the first dance is for Janitis." Baruta reddened in his face. "This time you will do as you are told and dance with Jambuloo. Janitis, ha, ha, what are you thinking about?"

"Then I will not dance at all."

"What are you doing, trying to embarrass me."

"This is important to me, Dad," replied Marquita, tears in her eyes. "I—"

"And so it is to me, you will do as you are told."

"No dancing for me, I now want to go home."

"You will do what you need to do, Marquita."

"Yes, I will dance with Janitis or not at all. You will have to drag me to the floor and I will dance as badly as I can if you force me."

All at once Baruta recognised a strength and stubbornness in Marquita, that he could not overcome here and now. He realised that she was determined and would make a disastrous scene if she did not get her way. Years of practice in dealing with tricky situations made him calm down in an instant. "Okay then, so it will be, I hope he has the skill."

"Plenty of skill in Janitis, but don't expect him to outshine others on the floor when it comes to dancing."

Baruta sighed. Janitis had been like a constant friend to Breer and Marquita, more so to her. He had been a constant visitor to their house. Breer was three years older and Janitis looked up to him. But Marquita had spent most of her time away from home with Janitis.

"I should have stopped it years ago," mumbled Baruta. "I never saw this coming. Silly girl."

Janitis was pleased and encouraged when he led Marquita to the floor. It was taboo to speak during the first dance. But Marquita managed to whisper, trying to move her lips as little as possible, to let Janitis know that this did by no means meant Baruta's approval, only her stubbornness.

During the first dance the Inner Six and their entourage were following the dancers intently, exchanging some comments between each other. The Upper Host sat separate on a raised platform, looking uninvolved. The spokesman for the Six stood up. All fell quiet now.

"It pleases the joint supervisors to announce and declare, that without any hesitation and doubt we have selected as the future bride for the Upper Host, the most beautiful and delightful and talented Marquita, daughter of Baruta the Magnificent and Mariote, his graceful partner." He held up the silver tiara set with precious stones, expecting Marquita to come forward and be crowned. Marquita's first reaction was disbelief, followed by shock so severe that she fainted and slid down on the floor.

Baruta's face portrayed a mixture of amazement and utter delight, while all around clapped, and Marquita still unconscious was carried to the dais to be crowned. When she came to, she mechanically turned to the panel, bowed, and barely audibly said, "You have chosen the wrong girl," which caused some subdued laughter.

3
The Chosen One

She dreamed of Janitis during the day and at night when she was asleep. She remembered their childish play, the vows they had made to each other. Their joined discoveries, many and varied. Discoveries of hidden features in the landscape, the hiding holes where furry nocturnal animals slept during the days. Discoveries of many fascinating birds, the way they moved through the air, some flapping their wings fast and vigorously, others just smoothly and elegantly gliding, apparently effortless. The discoveries of themselves and each other. And the discovery that they were in love, even though they were only children.

It had culminated one day, late afternoon, when the sun was low in the sky, the shadows long and the air mild and moist. All at once she had turned to face him, looking into his eyes and without a single word gently kissed him on his lips. Moving back just a little she had said, "I love you, Janitis."

And after a slight pause, he said hesitantly, "I will marry you," then repeated more forcefully, "As soon as we are old enough, I am going to marry you."

She had smiled and said, "Yes, of course that is what we will do, and we will have children."

Now all that seemed lost and impossible. Rebellion had solidly taken hold of her and she steadfastly refused to show any pleasure in her now exalted status, to the disappointment and annoyance of her parents, particularly her father, whose praises and presents were received without any sign of gratitude.

She tried to think of ways to escape her fate now clearly laid out before her and explained to her with great enthusiasm. This was not rewarded by any indication of pleasure, quite the opposite. She who had always been so full of joy and happiness was now sullen, showing no interest in anything and only wanting to sleep. Beautiful presents and the nicest of dresses were received with an even faced 'thank you', which did not convey any thankfulness at all. She dreamed all the time of ways to escape her fate but could not come up with anything practical. Refusing was not a possibility. What she was doing now was only making everybody annoyed, thinking of her as an ungrateful spoiled brat. Her close relationship with her dad, which had been such a great source of happiness to them both had now soured into feelings of mutual distrust.

Mother Mariotte had a gentle talk with her. It did not change Marquita's feelings one little bit, but it made her realise that her best chance of escape would be grounded in acting as if she was happy with her lot, while plotting some way out. How, she could not see now, but she decided to keep fighting and at the same time deceiving one and all. She was not by nature devious, not one little bit, but she had to employ every bit of deviousness if it could help to free herself from this fate. The thought of being betrothed to the Upper Host, to that ponderous old man, made her nauseous. To be publicly defiled on the alter that once served to rip the heart out of virgins, would do the same to her; if no longer in the literal sense, it would certainly turn her heart into stone.

Mum Mariotte went away feeling pleased, convinced she had managed to convert Marquita from being obstreperous into a once again cooperative daughter. What it had done was convert her from a sullen victim into an active combatant. First thing to do was get a message to Janitis to let him know she was not just passively giving in and that she would do all she could to honour her earlier vows to him.

From here on Marquita seemed like a changed girl. She spent lots of time in the library, reading history mainly and taking out stacks of books with her to read back at home. It was refreshing to her parents to see that she was trying to educate herself in preparation for her new position in life. Her zest was obviously back, she acted with purpose and dedication to her learning.

Marquita had hope, which motivated her, hope and determination to succeed in her aim. She read and reread the accounts of Estabella's escape. Estabella, who as the Chosen One would have her heart ripped out on the altar, as a sacrifice to the gods of fertility, but had managed to escape her fate. *If Estabella could do it, so can I*, was her reasoning. There was little time. In two weeks, she would be conveyed to Super Castle; she must have her plan laid out before then, and she needed Janitis's help.

She had to get a message to him, but who could she trust? No one. The servants who loved and cared for her, would be loyal to her parents and especially now, would report anything unusual to them. Her brother Breer, perhaps, he loved her dearly, and was not necessarily as impressed with his dad as Dad believed and most people thought. Then she could try and work a trick. There was the doll, she still had it, and it may serve the purpose. When they were still very young, in a moment of childish admiration Janitis had made a wooden doll for Marquita, while his mother, highly amused with his childish infatuation, had made a dress for it. Now she could have the doll returned with the excuse that she wanted to make it clear to Janitis that in her present elevated situation the doll was a childish embarrassment, and attach a hidden message. This was not as impossible as it may seem. They had played a game of developing a secret language, not looking like a script but as a decorative embellishment.

When Marquita gave the doll to Breer, her beloved brother, he looked at it bemused, then at Marquita, raising his eyebrows. "There is more to this than meets the eye," he murmured. "That funny scribbling must mean something," he said, looking at the secret language symbols along the hem of the dress.

Marquita was terribly disappointed at her plot being seen through immediately. She had thought it a perfect disguise of sorts, and here was Breer being suspicious immediately.

"No," he said, "do not worry, you did show me this doll when you got it, you were a small child then and so endeared with it and I happen to remember that it had not that peculiar decoration at the hem. A message to Janitis no doubt, but as I am your friend and his, no one will know and I don't want to know what the message says. I am your only bridge between yourself and Janitis, anyone else will straight away report anything unusual to Mum and Dad. I am sure you know that."

Marquita nodded silently.

"See, you are now all at once very special, you are royalty, on a different plain to any of us, higher than Mum or Dad. And they all see you as such. All except for me and Janitis. To us you are just Marquita, no more, no less."

Marquita started to cry silently, the only time she had shown emotion since the announcement.

"Don't worry, sis," Breer said somewhat roughly, then more softly, "Do not worry. I won't do anything behind your back. At least me you can trust and Janitis, but he is now out of reach for you. I will give him the doll, and give you his reply. I expect there will be one. But I must go now, and we probably should take more care in future, in case of ears listening at cracks in the wall."

Breer turned quickly and left, not looking back. Marquita crying unsettled him, he had not seen that happen since she was a toddler.

When Janitis received the message, he quickly deciphered it. Looking up, he saw Breer's back, who was already a distance away disappearing fast. Janitis sighed, not even a chance to thank him properly. He realised that Breer had not wanted Janitis to feel that he must explain anything the message might hold. The message just said 'Undress me'. Taking the doll's dress off, he found it had now a paper under garment, covered with scribbles, which took Janitis some time to fully decipher.

'No matter what you may hear now, tomorrow, the day after, etc, what they say of me, don't believe. I am yours and nobody else's. Do as I say. Read Estabella's escape. I will do the same. Use initiative. Prepare both bridges for burning. Burn east bridge when you judge I might try to escape, to create a distraction. Burn second bridge as soon as I am over it. At some time, I will join you at mystery destination past the ridge, or at our secret place. For ever yours Marquita.'

4
Super Castle

A few days later the escort arrived to convey Marquita to Super Castle. The carriage to take her across was festooned with flowers, the outriders dressed in red jackets and bright blue trousers. It looked all festive, but Marquita felt imprisoned and knew that she was. She managed to hide her despondency by thinking of her planned escape and reassuring herself that her plan, Estabella's plan, would succeed.

Mum Mariotte who had gone earlier to Marquita, to ensure that she was festively dressed for the occasion, guided her from the apartment to the carriage. When stepping outside Marquita faced the footmen as well as the smiling assembly of Sherba, Tintilla, Jansino and her dad.

Marquita would not look at them, turned to her mum, briefly embraced her and with a dismissive wave, aided by a footman, stepped in the carriage. She then turned and looked unsmilingly at the little group, their smiles frozen on their faces. Marquita could not look anyone in the face, especially not her dad. Neither Janitis or Breer were there.

She gave another casual wave, turned to look straight ahead, and the carriage set in motion. It moved slowly, so people assembled here and there could see the Chosen One travelling towards her destination.

Act as if you're happy, Marquita admonished herself. She forced herself to smile now and again and waved at small groups by the roadside.

Arriving at Super Castle she saw a line of staff ready to welcome her. A footman opened the carriage door, lowered the steps and supported her by the arm as she stepped down. There she was faced by the present Upper Host's wife, whom she soon would replace.

She wore a long lose fitting dress, to hide her advanced pregnancy.

She inclined her head. "Welcome, Chosen One", extending both hands, to briefly touch Marquita.

"Thank you, Your Highness", Marquita responded mechanically. "I appreciate your friendly welcome."

On her way to her apartment, she was introduced to the line of respectfully smiling staff then entered a large hall, with an impressive semicircular stairway leading up to her rooms.

Her accommodation in Super Castle was superb, a large room with windows giving a wide view over the town and the country beyond. Heavy metal grills before the windows prevented the possibility of escape. The living area was spacious and well-furnished with an old-fashioned opulence. The sidewall opposite the windows had two wide arches, no doors, but curtains which were open on her arrival. Each room had a comfortable bed in it. One room was colourfully decorated, the other more austere.

Her constant companion as it turned out to be, was waiting for her inside. She was a woman of comfortable proportions, middle aged, exhibiting a good nature with an open pleasant smile and addressing her alternately as 'my child' and 'Your Highness'. Over her dress she carried a leather belt, fixed around the middle, secured with a strap over her left shoulder and carrying a ring with a bunch of keys, some of old-fashioned size, meant for Super Castle locks. She moved with an easy grace and when Marquita was shown in, put her arm around her, saying, "Come in, my child. This is your accommodation from now till the big day, when you will move to the Super quarters. But you will be very comfortable here, Your Highness."

Marquita surveyed her surroundings. Apart from the door they had entered, there were the arches giving access to the bedrooms, another door in the side between the two arches and a very heavy door with large metal hinges at the northern wall, adjoining a large fireplace.

"I am your companion from today onwards till the big celebration, anything you need or want just ask me. My name is Ariotto, I am often referred to as Sister Ariotto, or just Sister or just Ariotto, you please yourself, Your Highness, call me what you like, I am your companion and servant."

And prison guard, mused Marquita.

"Anything you want just ask me," she repeated." She saw Marquita surveying the room, focusing on the two closed doors. "Oh, that one in between our rooms is the bathroom. Here is where you will sleep," she said, taking her by the hand and leading her to the nicest of the two bedrooms, "and that is where I sleep," pointing out the other one.

Marquita's eyes involuntarily went to the door at the far end. "And what is that?" she said when she noticed that Ariotto had followed her gaze. "Something very valuable must be hidden there," she added portraying innocent ignorance. "Can you open that?"

"Oh that, no that is of historical interest only. It leads through a long dark corridor, a ramp sloping down to the outside. It was Estabella's escape way, of no interest now. You know the story, of course."

"Well, we were told in school about Estabella, so I know she escaped up north. But how did she open this enormous door?"

"She took the key off her keeper, who carried it on her key ring, like I do now." She indicated the largest of the keys hanging by her side.

Marquita laughed. "Will it still work?"

"I expect so, never tried."

"Well try."

"Why?"

"Why not?"

"Ah, well okay." Ariotto walked up to the door inserted the key, and managed to turn it, having to use some force. She could, with some effort, open the door a little. It squeaked loudly on its hinges. Marquita tried to look in but only saw darkness and a musty smell hit her in the face, invading the room.

"Creepy," she said, thinking, *I'd better try and get some oil on those hinges.*

"I seem to remember that there was also a door at the other end," she remarked, trying to look innocent.

"Yes," Ariotto quite happily replied, "but that one is opened from the outside. It does not need a key from the inside, that way Estabella could escape."

Thank you, Ariotta, Maquita thought, doing her best to look totally indifferent. *This apparently innocent soul could be of great help to me,* she reflected. *She is so lovely and simple by all appearances.*

"Oh," Ariotto said looking very worried, "I totally forgot, that key was for ceremonial purposes only, I was clearly told, never to use the big key. Ah, Your Highness, please never tell anyone I opened that door, I will be in so much trouble and I have always done the right thing up here, that is why I was given this job. It's a big honour you know. Please, darling, never tell anyone."

Marquita smiled. "Rest assured, Sister Ariotto I never will. That is a solemn promise."

The food was simply beautiful and anything Marquita asked for was supplied as soon as it could be procured. After dinner, sitting about with Ariotto, Marquita started to fish into her background. The more she knew, the easier it may be to deceive her and find a means to get the key off her to unlock the big door in the back wall. Most of what she was told, just confirmed matters she already had learned from studying the library's books. After dinner they just sat and talked. Ariotto was happy enough to reminisce in the presence of this happy and attentive girl. She had enough to be happy about, she reflected. Ceremoniously and publicly being deflowered may be a concern to any or at least many girls, but after that was over and done with, it was all glory and good living from there on.

"How did you manage to get a position at Super Castle?" enquired Marquita. "Jobs here would be very much sought after."

"Ah, well, after I got my basic carer's qualifications I stayed for many years with the Sisters of Support, an order that for no benefit to themselves helps those in need. We provided for ourselves doing market gardening, selling surpluses at the markets and we also received some generous donations. But most of our time was spent helping others less fortunate unable to look after themselves properly, cleaning the places of old and disabled people, comforting the very ill and dying and whatever came our way.

"Then there came this request from Super Castle for a sister in aid. This is very much an easy honorary position, and the sisters try to grant something easy for anyone who has served over twenty years with a good record. This I had done. Being a Sister of Support is very demanding. Apart from providing for ourselves we spend long hours looking after those that need looking after. It is at times tiring. When I got the position here it proved to be such an easy life, and now they have honoured me again by letting me help the Chosen One.

"But before I got this assignment I at times found the easy time here not all that easy after all. As a Sister of Support you are always busy, you work hard from morning till night. It seems strange but after some time I found it difficult to have so much leisure time. I was longing for someone to need me, someone to ask me for help. So now I am very happy to be given the task to look after you. I do not want to sound ungrateful because my life has been so easy here, the company very pleasant, thoughtful and intelligent, but I still miss the constant Involvement with people who are in need. I started to drink a drop of sweet sherry now and again, maybe more than a drop, so I have stopped that, only having a drink on special occasions. You like sweet sherry?"

"Oh yes, I like it very much," Marquita lied, because apart from knowing that it was an alcoholic drink, she did not know the first thing about it, never had tasted it as a matter of fact. "Let's have some tomorrow after dinner," she suggested. "That will be nice when we sit talking, after all this is a very special occasion, don't you think?"

"Mmm... yes," Ariotto hesitated, "but I cannot drink too much, it is treacherous, if you have one glass you always want another one, and then it can become hard to stop."

"Just ask for a bottle," Marquita ventured, "and each day we have one glass each after dinner while we sit here talking."

Next day they finished dinner just as daylight started to fade. Ariotto got up, lit the candles, filling the room with a cosy atmosphere.

"Time for our sherry, Ariotto," ventured Marquita.

"I just have a small one," Ariotto replied, then found two small glasses, and half-filled each. The candles reflected in the yellow liquid in the glasses.

"Cheers." Marquita lifted her glass, looking Ariotto in the eye with a happy smile, then took a careful sip, not knowing what to expect, as she had never had alcohol before, except for a small amount of diluted light wine. The sting burned her tongue and throat and brought tears to her eyes.

Fortunately, Ariotto had not noticed her discomfort, enjoying the taste of her favourite drink. "Mmm," she hummed, "very nice, this is a superb sherry."

"Yes, excellent," Marquita replied, staging a quick recovery from an unexpected experience. "Yes, very good." *Take it easy*, she thought, *no need to hurry things*, but she could not help noticing that Ariotto finished her drink soon, unable to keep her eyes off the glass, then having a look at the bottle, but not pouring herself a second one, not on that first night.

With dinner Marquita requested some extra oil and vinegar, and when Ariotto went to the bathroom, made use of her absence to lubricate the hinges of the exit door liberally.

The night after, having chatted cosily for a while, Marquita refilled Ariotto's glass. "Might as well have a little more."

"What about yourself?" asked Ariotto.

"As soon as I have finished it, I too will have another one," she replied, smiling.

Before long Ariotto, having finished her third glass, looked longingly at the bottle.

"Ah, just one last nightcap," Marquita suggested.

Ariotto almost unperceivably nodded, and after downing that one said, "I will have a snooze now," and disappeared to her room, where she stumbled over the mat and fell on the bed. She took off her key belt, dropped it on the floor, removed her robe and slid under the blanket, snoring loudly after five minutes.

Marquita deliberated for a few moments, then stealthily took hold of the heavy key and the belt, took one more look at Ariotto, and noiselessly moved to the exit door. She inserted the key and had trouble turning it. Succeeding at long last, she hurried back with the belt and keys to Ariotto's room and put it down on the floor.

Unexpectedly Ariotto sat up. "What are you doing here?" she asked, now looking very suspicious.

"Just checking if you were all right, Ariotto."

"It's my job to look after you, not your job to look after me," came the unusually assertive reply, "don't forget." Then she laid back down and was asleep again in seconds.

The next night after a few sherries Ariotto was in an expansive mood and happily talking away about the history of Super Castle, when Marquita managed to steer the discussion toward the castle's security, the position of the guards and the arrangements for the re-enactment. Most of this she had learned from her reading, but she wanted confirmation to make sure that things were still being done the way she assumed. She had to get Ariotto talking about those things without raising suspicion, or giving the impression that she was trying to find out the security on the last night.

"There are guards in the guard house, every night, and near all exits and entries. Why I do not know, it's just always been that way, but on re-enactment night many of the guards have the night off, to be ready for the next early morning start. The guards remaining are having a barbecue and drinks nearby, and a white horse is tied up to a post, that signifies the horse on which Estabella escaped. Not the same horse of course, that was fifty years ago. This time, because it is fifty years, it will be on a large scale."

Ariotto silently fingered her glass, turning it around and around, then continued. "After Estabella's escape the ceremony of sacrificing the Chosen One was eliminated. Instead, the Inner Six ruled that the Chosen One would be the virgin bride of the Upper Host, be his wife and escort for two years, when the next one would be selected.

"After ten years, the next generation, now thoroughly disgusted by the previous discontinued barbaric custom, decided on a celebration of Estabella's escape. It was such a success that it continued year after year.

"Most of the guards get the night off the night before, to prepare for celebration day, and the ones left are having drinks here nearby to celebrate the re-enactment."

So, Marquita thought, she had chosen right to plan her escape for the last night. First there would be a horse, then secondly the guards might be inebriated. All the same it was a tricky affair. She had to get rid of Ariotto at dusk or soon after, signal Janitis, and hopefully he would be ready to do his job. Ariotto's liking for drink would be the biggest help, but she had to find out what, if any, special arrangements there were as far as she was concerned for the last night. "Only three nights to go, Ariotto, I will miss our pleasant talks."

"No, no, you will have bigger experiences ahead instead of conversing with an old nurse."

"But we must make the most of the nights left and do something special on the last one. So far, we made a big hole in that bottle of sweet sherry. I have heard that something called port makes a very good after dinner drink, maybe we should get some of that, what do you reckon, Ariotto?"

"Don't know, I think sweet sherry is just perfect, but I will order a bottle of port if you like."

"And something special for the last night?"

"Well, there already is something special for the last night, it's in the healing cupboard in the bathroom." Ariotto pointed at the little key on her key ring. "But that's something for you to drink sometime after dinner on the last night. I have very definite instructions to do that."

She had to get hold of that bottle before the fateful night, but how? She needed to get her hands on that little key, but it was risky business. "It's a lovely little key," she said, "can I have a look at it?" It looked very ordinary in shape, but still essential to open that cupboard. She did not think she had the skill to work the lock with a bit of wire, anyway she did not have any wire. She needed to get hold of that key long enough to open that cupboard, empty that bottle and replace the contents with something else. She could not see any alternative but to try the same trick she had used for the big key, only this time she had to get the little key off the ring as it would be impossible to use the little key with the weight of the belt and the other keys.

First, she managed to convince Ariotto to order a bottle of port, being a desirable after dinner drink. A sherry before dinner and port after, Marquita argued.

Ariotto was soon convinced of that procedure. The sherry before dinner went down well, then for the port after.

"Well, that's quite pleasant too," Ariotto agreed, and had a few more. But this time she showed no sign of retiring.

Marquita started to panic. Somehow or other she had to get hold of that little key. She would have to wait till Ariotto was asleep, and then try to remove it from the ring. She had to do it this night or the next so she could replace the contents before the final night. This time Ariotto did not seem to be in a hurry to go to bed, so Marquita suggested, "We might as well have another one," tossing her own drink into one of the decorative vases while Ariotto was spending time in the bathroom. There was only tonight and tomorrow night to act. She had to replace whatever was in the cupboard that belonged to the little key with something innocuous. It was clear from what Ariotto had divulged that whatever it was she was going to get was a sedative of some sort. It would render her incapable of decisive appropriate action. She had to get hold of that little key, somehow or other, as soon as possible.

Ariotto came back from the bathroom and found her little glass filled again. The red-brown liquid shone temptingly in the candlelight. She hesitated for a moment, drank half of it, then drained the glass. "Bedtime," she said, with a heavy drawl, and disappeared, dropping down on her bed without removing either belt or gown.

Marquita decanted her glass back into the bottle, then started to observe Ariotto. On the pretence of helping her to be comfortable, she started to act as if removing the key belt, trying her hardest to get the small key off the ring. It was attached to the main ring by a smaller split ring which she managed to open and remove. Not wanting to waste time, she grabbed the sherry bottle, which still had a small amount in it, and disappeared into the bathroom. It took minutes to unlock the little cupboard where among other medical matters she found a small bottle, containing some kind of draught, labelled 'For the Chosen One, to be taken after dinner the night before the big event'. She removed the stopper and poured its contents into the sherry bottle, then filled it with water, replacing it, then closing and locking the cupboard. She heard noises out of Ariotto's bedroom, quickly put the sherry on the table, and hurried into Ariotto's alcove.

Ariotto sat on the bed, looking dazed and worried, holding her key ring in her hand, murmuring, "It's gone, it's gone."

"What's gone?" Marquita asked. "What are you talking about, you lost something?"

"My little key, it's no longer there, look."

Marquita took the ring, said with a puzzled intonation, "That's peculiar, I saw it there myself this afternoon, I'm sure of that, it must have worked its way off when you went to bed, let's have a look." Bending over with her face close to the ground, she made a scooping movement with her hand over the floor. "See, here it is, it was laying on the ground here next to your bed. Lucky that I found it so quickly. Will I put it back on for you?"

"Please do, oh good you found it," Ariotto sighed. "I need some more sleep." Marquita replaced the ring with the tiny key on it. Ariotto turned on her side and was snoring in no time at all.

5
Escape

The final night. Marquita was tense like a tightly wound spring. She had made all the preparations successfully, now it was a matter of executing all, nothing must go wrong. So far, she had believed in success without ever doubting it. But this was it, all at once so unbelievably close. She breathed deeply to control the nerves, but she had trouble not to shake when she poured Ariotto a generous helping of what was left in the sherry bottle, saying, "I will stick to port this time, I've done with sherry. Cheers," lifting her glass and looking at Ariotto. They both took a swig, Marquita a tiny one, Ariotto emptying almost half of her glass, with the first gulp.

She looked puzzled. "This sherry tastes different from usual, but very nice all the same, have a taste."

"No, thanks, Ariotto, it will be port for me tonight. I know well enough what the sherry tastes like."

"Mmmm, it tastes different but very nice all the same."

"Well, one's taste is not always the same you know," ventured Marquita. "Depends what you ate or drank before. It's the same sherry out of the same bottle, must be your imagination."

"Oh, it's time for your potion, I almost forgot. That would have landed me in trouble." Ariotto started to fiddle with the keys and after a while managed to get the little one off and went to the bathroom to get the bottle with the supposed drug. She came back with a smile on her face. "Oh, you haven't finished your port yet, drink it up, and I will give you this."

"Just pour it in another glass, Ariotto, I will have that first so we can't forget and I will drink the port later." Marquita finished the proffered drink in two quick gulps, exclaiming after the first swallow, "Oh, this is really beautiful," than quickly downing the rest.

So far so good. Dinner was brought in and in no time at all they both started to eat eagerly. It was not just excellent, it was absolutely superb. In between the main course and dessert Ariotto downed the rest of her drink. Marquita quickly refilled it. That emptied the sherry bottle.

Dessert was sweet and delicious with a slight alcoholic tinge. When it was brought in Marquita asked the servant to be back for the empty containers in not more than ten minutes as they both were having an early night. The servant nodded understandingly, while Marquita managed to exchange her full port glass for Ariotto's empty one.

"Oh, you drank it at last," Ariotto exclaimed on her return from the bathroom. "I thought you were going to sit on it all night."

"Not me, not likely, and I poured you one too, it's a good thing to finish with port. Ah well, I might as well have another one to keep you company," and poured herself a glass full, smiling broadly.

Ariotto took a swig. "Nice, but not as nice as today's sherry, I could ask for another bottle, I suppose."

"No, let's stick with the port."

Ariotto looked doubtful than started a farewell talk, thought up before, but now half forgotten. "Marquita, highnezzz... it'zz been a pwiveliidgge to hhawing veenn your zerwanst and gompagnnion..." She swallowed a few times, nodded and closed her eyes.

"Thank you very much for your kind words and great companionship this week, I could not have wished for better care. I will never forget this. Come, I will help you to bed."

Momentarily Ariotto woke with a level of alertness. "No all wongg, iz me who muz you elp doo bed."

"Later, after you have rested for a while, now let me help you."

She supported Ariotto to her bed where she fell asleep immediately. Marquita closed the curtain to Ariotto's bed chamber. It was getting darker, and she contemplated for a while, looking out of the window. She could hear some boisterous noises; the guards were as it seemed, having a good time filling themselves with beer or wine or both. *Now is the time*, she decided, took the largest of three candles, then put it down again. *I might need a weapon.* Looking around, her eyes connected with one of the irons hanging near the fireplace, a metal rod, with a curved bit at one end. She grabbed it and hung it inside her dress, the curved bit over her collar. It felt uncomfortable but gave her a sense of security. She picked up the candle again, went to the window, making their secret childhood sign, the J M twice, hoping that Janitis would see it.

Needing both hands to open the exit door, she put the candle briefly on the floor. In spite of the oil she had put on the hinges, they still squeaked alarmingly. With her back against the door, she managed to keep it open long enough to grab the candle than slowly let go of it and made her way down along the dark musty corridor. She proceeded slowly, some vague dread stopping her from hurrying.

Arriving at the lower end, it was easy enough to open the bottom door by pressing down on a large bar running across it. She pushed the door open carefully and immediately saw what she had hoped for. In the distance to the right the horizon was illuminated by an orange glow. *Ah, Janitis,* she thought, *you have seen my sign and done your job. You marvellous man.*

Silhouetted against the distant glow were the backs of the guardsmen, being totally absorbed by the puzzling spectacle. Marquita could not believe her luck. Quietly and silently, she extinguished the candle and let the door shut by its own weight, controlling it with her left hand. Some distance ahead and slightly to her left stood the big white stallion loosely tied to a post. She made her way forward, untied the horse, mounted it and gave it a slap on the back, whispering, "Hoi!" in its ear. The horse leapt forward and fell into an easy canter.

Looking back at the guards she noticed one of them looking back in her direction and yelling out, "Hey!" Then she went forward on the moonlit path leading north, her only way of escape.

6
Janitis

Janitis wore a dark fibre hat, pulled down to conceal the shape of his head, but not so low that he couldn't see comfortably. He had shaped himself a beard and moustache to make him completely unrecognisable. He just looked like an old man. His horse, Sniffer, had its hooves wrapped in bits of blanket, to dampen the sound where they had to cross pavement or rocky ledges. He knew he could not run a risk. He knew what to do. He had studied Estabella's escape in great detail.

To duplicate that was Marquita's aim. He had, days before, stacked dry wood, tinder bark and some larger branches underneath the bridges on both ends. The lighting of the second bridge was straightforward. As soon as Marquita had crossed, he would light it. When to light the first one was more critical. Too early and the guards' attention would be back on their job, too late was no use at all, except that the pursuers would not be able to use it as an alternative crossing. The best time would be just before Marquita would open the outside door to mount her waiting horse. He knew she would try to give a sign, but would she have a chance? And what would the sign be. It must come from one of the windows where she was detained. As soon as it began to darken Janitis started on his journey, skirting the settled area, avoiding pavement and people. He could not set out in daylight for fear of being seen. As a result, he had to hurry, because Marquita would try to imitate Estabella and wait for darkness to act, but she would also have to act on whatever opportunity would arise. It was therefore important that Janitis was in position as quickly as possible after dark.

Moving through the bush was not always as quiet as he had hoped; sometimes Sniffer stepped on a branch which would crack noisily, sometimes sleeping birds would wake up protesting loudly. It took Janitis and Sniffer almost half an hour to reach east bridge. He settled down and looked at Super Castle. After a while he could vaguely discern the outline of the windows. It was a long way off. Sniffer stood quietly aside; it seemed as if he was aware of the need to make no noise. Janitis loved that horse. Concentrating hard on the windows he became less and less aware of his surroundings, the gurgling of the water where it forced through a narrowing in the creek bed followed by a sharp turn in its course. His eyes started to water from the continuous strain of focussing on something hardly visible, maybe partly imagined.

He had worried about being too late. Maybe he had been, but he did not think so. He had been here now for a long time, with no sign given, but she had to wait for an opportunity. Would it arise? It could be much longer still. Sniffer next to him was facing the same direction as if looking with him and for him. Funny horse. Then, all at once there it was. Their secret sign drawn with the light of a candle. A big J, then some up and downs, close enough for an M, twice. Janitis was full of life and energy now. He decided to give it some time, but not much, before lighting the fire. The fire would ignite quickly, he reasoned, how soon would the guards notice it? How long would it take Marquita from doing her candle act to reach the bottom door and open it? That was the time the guards should be distracted.

Too many unknowns. He decided to count to ten, then started to worry how long it would take till they would notice the fire, decided on five instead, but actually lit it at three. It took very quickly and the flames shot up. He stepped back from the light of the fire which was throwing a hot glow on his face, took Sniffer's reins, led him away a few steps, mounted, and cantered towards west bridge. Now it was on, his heart was pounding, he could hear all the noise he and Sniffer were making, and now distinctly heard some screams coming from the direction of the castle.

7
Chase

All had gone better than she could have hoped for. When moving through the door to the outside she looked at the backs of the guards staring at a distant fire. She grinned, satisfied. *Ah, Janitis, you have done your job and did it well.* But the squeaking of the closing door drew the attention of one of the regiment's guards, the somewhat diminutive weirdo Wally. An unusual name for an unusual fellow. He observed her with disbelief. That looked like Marquita, the Chosen One, Janitis' friend in times past, but now the bride of the Superior One, what was she doing here? His delay in acting gave Marquita the opportunity to untie her white stallion, mount it and take off as fast as she could. "Hi, see that," said Wally, with disbelief, "that was her, Marquita the Chosen One taking off as fast as she can."

Most of the group reluctantly disengaged from the fiery spectacle on the horizon, and with a mixture of annoyance and impatience, turned to see what silly Wally was on about, and noticing the stallion gone, looked at him, enquiring, "What?" in various voices. "What happened?"

"It was her, Marquita the Chosen One, taking off on the big white one."

Disbelief made place for panic, orders were given, horses mounted and all took off in pursuit, direction north, the path to west bridge. This was the only logical way she could be going, unless she would return to the village, but the sound of the heavy hooves of the big stallion clearly gave the direction toward the bridge.

Marculas, the commander of this purely conventional replay of Estabella's escape, an appointment of honour and appreciation of past services, tried to come to grips with the situation. Was this just an extension of the play-acting, or was it for real? Silly Wally said he had seen her and was sure it was Marquita; if he was right this was not just serious, but extremely very serious.

His brain was clouded by the heavy drinking they were still involved in at the time the fire started, which surely was east bridge going up in flames. What was going on? But it should not be difficult to catch up with the escapee, if it was Marquita on the white stallion. The guardsmen were all on their own fast horses, while the white stallion was more bulk than speed. And she had only a few minutes start on them, maybe five or a little more. They should catch up with her at west bridge or before, he calculated.

It seemed to take his men too much time to get onto their mounts, some being the worst for wear because they had been drinking continuously for some time now.

"Come on, get moving," he shouted. "You, Jaculo, get going," he yelled at the youngest of the group who also had the fastest horse. "Catch up with her and stop her."

The whole band got underway. His first job was to catch up with her, no matter what. No matter if it was play-acting, or if Wally was right and it was the Chosen One fleeing. But why would she, being granted the biggest honour and privilege any young woman could hope for. It did not make any sense. Whatever happened, he had to handle this with care, because if it was Marquita, the Chosen One, he could not treat her as some escaped prisoner. She was the Chosen One, whatever he did he must treat her with respect. What would Jaculo do when he caught up with her? *I have not instructed him, Oh, by the Supreme Almighty, I hope he has good sense.*

Marquita was racing at full gallop. Just as well that she had some experience in bareback riding. She pressed her steed to maximum effort, knowing that her advantage was minimal and she must cross the bridge before they caught up with her, because then all was lost. She also realised that her horse was not fast. By all means it was just a representation of the white stallion Estabella had escaped on, which according to the recorded story was a big heavy stallion called Fearless. So Marquita kept urging him on. "Come on, Fearless save me, please save me," and she believed then that he understood and did his utmost to get her to safety.

Hanging onto his mane, her knees pressed into his sides, she encouraged him to go faster by beating a rhythm with her feet on his rump. But this horse was more suited for pulling a cart or drawing a plough through a field than racing with the guards. The solid iron she had secured from the fireplace hung under her dress on her back, so she could reach it from alongside her neck, the way Janitis carried his sword, but while Janitis's sword was in a sheath, hers rubbed against her back. Why had she taken it? She wanted some kind of weapon as she was determined not to be taken. She would not be taken.

"I will not be taken," she kept repeating to herself. "No matter what it takes I will fight like a wild cat."

The night was quiet, apart from the heavy thumping of the horse's broad feet, and her own breathing which ran heavy as if she herself was doing all the heavy work instead of Fearless. The fast rhythm of another horse, the one pursuing her, sounded light and far away but gaining on her steadily. She could tell from the loudness of the sound.

She could hear the pounding of hooves getting closer and closer. The rhythm was faster than her horse could achieve. Then the moment for panic arrived. She knew all was lost as the leading steed of the pursuer sounded not more than fifty or a hundred metres behind her while she also heard others further in the distance. The bridge, the only structure that could save her, was still hundreds of metres away, there was no way she could make it.

Her pursuer kept gaining on her until he was only metres behind her and in an act of desperation, she threw her scarf at Jaculo's face, temporary blinding him, but he brushed it aside and though having lost some distance now started to catch up again. With her right hand she took hold of the iron rod, pulling it from behind her, determined to hit her pursuer across the face when he drew level with her.

It would be a very long time before Marquita would know what caused the next events. Her first thoughts were of Janitis having done something courageous and clever, but the truth of the event would not be clear to her for some years. When she was sure that all was lost the sound of a devastating crash behind her stopped the pursuing hoofbeats, and agonising screams from man and beast tore through the night. The more distant hoof beats stopped soon, for a few minutes, then shouts from Marculas urged his men on, and the pursuit continued.

But Marquita had gained some time, enough maybe to cross the bridge and hopefully enough time between them for Janitis to stop her pursuers.

8
Breer

At the announcement of the Chosen One, Breer had been shocked to the core.

While his family was celebrating, his first thought was for Janitis. When he spotted his face drawn in despair between all the happy laughter and congratulations, he wanted to go up to him and say something, put his arm around him to comfort him, but he did not know what to say. They had never hugged or shown any affection that way. They were just good friends, and they both knew it. Now Breer stood there perplexed, staring at Janitis. Janitis looked up, expressionless, then turned and made for the exit. Since then, Janitis had avoided all contact with the Baruta household.

Five days before the marriage Marquita was transferred to Super Castle. Since then, Breer spent little time at home. He came there to eat and sleep, was sullen and uncommunicative. He found it impossible to cope with their excitement about the honour that had come to the family. He suffered because he knew Marquita and Janitis were hurting. This was in sharp contrast to Baruta who was all smiles and enthusiasm. Baruta found it difficult to come to grips with Breer's attitude and the fact that Janitis, who had always been so close as to be considered part of the family, had not even shown up to offer his congratulations.

"Why are you so down in the mouth, why are you not joining us celebrating your sister being the Chosen One?" he confronted Breer.

"Because my sister is not celebrating either," Breer replied. "If she would be happy, I would be happy for her, but she is no longer with us and I am sad. And I won't come and see her being defiled by an old man."

"What!" Baruta's face showed the emotion of a man being stabbed with a dagger. "How dare you. And you will be there, that is an order." Breer got up from the table and walked out. "What is for heaven's sake the matter with everyone," exclaimed Baruta. "We reached the ultimate honour and we all should be proud. But I haven't seen Janitis around and Breer acts as if we suffered a calamity."

Breer had slept badly and walked as if in a daze. He attended to his garden mechanically, but without the pleasure it usually gave him. It was now the day before. In the morning he did a bit of weeding, then, instead of going home for lunch he took some of the ripe plums and cherries, ate without paying attention to the rich flavour, lay down in the shade, and as he had slept badly for many nights fell asleep and slept for hours. When he woke up it was late in the afternoon. He looked around, rubbed his eyes, got up and started to walk without a set plan. He had without giving it any thought headed in the direction of Janitis's parents' pastures. Reaching the edge of a forested area he now faced the large enclosure where Janitis's father kept his horses, including Janitis's personal horse Sniffer.

Breer leaned on the fence, his eyes staring into the distance. In the far distance he could just see their house. At times he had visited there, at other times he had met Janitis away from their house, but more often Janitis had been a visitor at their place, staying at times for an evening meal, when he and Marquita had been roaming the fields. Breer had a few friends his age, but spent most of his time in his garden, growing fruit and veggies with some flowering plants in between just because the look of that gave him a sense of satisfaction.

He sighed realising that he had come here, to be close to Janitis, but at the same time was frightened to meet him as he simply did not know what to say. He had always been like the older brother to Janitis, helping and advising him, but now he was devoid of any comforting or helpful words. He searched among the horses for Sniffer, spotted him and became transfixed by what seemed like a bearded man, his hat drawn down hiding half his face, tying something around Sniffer's hooves. He tensed and focussed. Sniffer seemed extremely compliant for a stranger to interfere with him. But that stranger had something familiar about him, then it hit home.

Stranger, stranger, no way, that was no stranger, that was Janitis, who had disguised himself and who was wrapping his horse's hooves with some kind of material, so it wouldn't make any noise on hard surfaces. But why, what was he up to? Did he have some madcap plan to rescue Marquita, for surely it must have something to do with her, why else would he do something obviously secret! Must keep an eye on him, whatever he was going to do, if it is too silly, he must try and prevent it.

As quickly as he could, Breer walked back to his family's stables and got Grapple, his own horse, saddled it and took a coil of rope off a peg and his stockwhip. He rode back through the forest, dismounted and led Grapple as silently as possible the last bit towards the fence. By now the sun was setting and he could, in the distance towards the other side of Janitis's parents' paddock, dimly see Janitis leading his horse into the woods in the direction of the river. *At least he's not aiming for Super Castle*, Breer reflected, still completely baffled by what was going on.

It would be very difficult to keep track of Janitis without giving away he was spying on him. Assuming that Janitis was heading towards the river then following it upstream, Breer followed a parallel course keeping under cover as much as possible. Soon he lost contact with Janitis. But as he moved on, he mulched over Marquita's frequent comments that Estabella had escaped her fate, and her admiration for that, and of all the people she would like to have a talk with, Estabella was on top of her list, that is after Janitis, she had added.

He also recalled that the books Marquita had taken from the library were all about the history of that time and at least one a straight recounting of Estabella's escape and how she had managed it. So that's what they are on about, he thought, a risky try, but he understood and even felt Marquita's foreboding at her so-called marriage to the Upper Host and losing Janitis. If it had not been for the tension he felt in his head and chest he could have appreciated this wonderful night, it being neither hot nor cold, and the rising full moon casting a transparent golden glow over the open land between the trees.

Breer sighed. The stillness in the air asked for a response, as if something had to happen. The atmosphere was full of expectation and Breer could not harmonise this with the peacefulness of his environment. Some urge made him look to the right when he saw the orange glow against the night sky. He immediately knew where and what it was, the bridge, the eastern bridge on fire. That must have been Janitis blocking off one of the avenues of pursuit, he assumed, so it was on, Marquita was trying her escape. She must take the west bridge and try to reach the Northland and find refuge with Estabella who she could expect to sympathise.

Breer straight away hurried to the track leading from Super Castle to west bridge. He knew for sure now that it was on. Marquita was doing what she had implied, she was making a run for it. He heard some shouting from the direction of Super Castle, then it was quiet for a while, followed by the heavy footfalls of a galloping horse. The rhythmic thumping was all that disturbed the quiet night for half a minute or so, then increased shouting and swearing. Soon on top of the heavy hoof beats, lighter and faster ones super-imposed. By the mercy of the Upper Host, she had done it, she had managed to make her escape, but her advantage was limited. She had to cross the bridge before they caught up with her. Breer just assumed that Janitis would have done something to prevent her followers getting over the bridge.

He got to the track about fifty metres before the bridge. In his mind there was no doubt now that it was Marquita being chased by the guard. He took the rope to connect it to a tree opposite to let the first horse pass and pull it straight after that so the chasing horse would fall when his legs hit the rope. Not enough time he realised, now in panic, not enough time. In despair he grabbed his whip, and while raising it saw Marquita flash by, Jaculo not more than ten metres behind and catching up. With a loud crack he brought the whip hard across the nose of Jaculo's mount, which reared, dislodging Jaculo, then shrieked and arched sideways in the bush. The sickening sound of disaster. A leg cracked with a dry sound, followed by the noise of crashing, while the horse shrieked again and landed with a thud.

Breer heard the rest of the pack approaching, quickly turned his steed and moved off as fast as possible, keeping under cover where he could. Janitis would have to take care of the rest, but he hoped his intervention would make it possible for Marquita to succeed.

Getting home he quietly stabled his horse, then entered through the back door after having removed his heavy boots, and tiptoed up the stairs to his bedroom. Going up he heard Jansino say to Sherba, "I thought I heard the backdoor being opened, but nothing there, but come and look, two fires near the bridges. I'd better wake up Breer, he will want to know what's going on."

Breer had quickly stripped and put on his night gear, pretending to be awoken from a deep sleep.

Quickly throwing a loose cloak over his pyjamas, rubbing pretend sleep out of his eyes, he reluctantly opened the bedroom door. Jansino's face expressed a mixture of urgency and bewilderment. "Sorry, Breer, to wake you, but there is something strange going on near the river somewhere near the bridges. I just went out by coincidence, thought I heard the backroom door opening but there was nothing there, I must be hearing things, but anyway, I then noticed these fires on the horizon, and it is not even the dry season. But come and see for yourself."

Breer just nodded and followed Jansino down the stairs. "Better put some clothes on and go and investigate," he said, being eager to visit the crime scene now that his alibi was established, taking care not to carry his whip this time.

The east bridge was still smouldering at the southern end as he approached, the northern side still throwing up flames into the sky. He savoured the smell of burning wood, then slowly followed the river towards the other bridge, which was still burning fiercely. *You did your best*, Janitis, he thought, *hope she got away safely*. It was quiet around the bridge, but he could hear the footfall of approaching riders from the direction of the village. It was Calli and Collo, twin brothers, who had been awake when they heard riders approaching. It was the posse that delivered Jaculo to the local sick bay. Hearing their brief summation, they decided to go and have a look for themselves, it all sounded too exciting not to.

They informed Breer how apparently Jaculo's mount had fallen for some unknown reason, broken a leg and had to be destroyed, what a pity such a beautiful animal and the fastest horse in the country. Why the horse had fallen was unclear. Jaculo was still unconscious when he was carried in. They all three went back to have a look where the horse had fallen, its carcass still lying next to the path. No one else there. It appeared that the posse bringing in Jaluco had not been able or willing to provide any more information, other than that something very funny was going on and if they wished to know more, they would have to wait for the return of Marculas.

The three rode silently back home deciding to try and get some sleep, if they could manage that after all the excitement.

Breer felt unexpectedly relaxed and had a few hours of solid sleep after having not experienced good sleep for the last two weeks.

It was still dark when he next woke up, refreshed and full of energy. He was sure that Marquita had made good her escape, although, could he be sure? He had seen no trace of the rest of the guard, they probably had forded the river higher up and continued their pursuit. But by then Marquita would have a considerable lead, and although her mount was anything but fast, it would have plenty of stamina and would be able to keep going for a long time. And there was Janitis, he would put obstacles in Marculas's way if he had the opportunity.

But where was Janitis, this side of the bridge or the other? This caused him great anxiety, for now his peace of mind was gone again. The burning of the bridges? Had Janitis expected to return to the village with an innocent look on his face? Stupid boy, that would never work. If Marquita had made good her escape, which he solidly believed, then who had burned the bridges? Breer could not think of anybody else that could be suspected of doing that, surely Janitis had to be if not the only suspect, then certainly suspect number one. *If he has any brains he must be on the other side, but that is not safe either, the Northland is not safe for men.* Northland's biggest safeguard against foreigners was its reputation, whether correct or incorrect, that they had the habit of castrating any man crossing their borders. Poor Janitis, he was in a no-win situation, his only saving could be to flee to Westland. Little was known about that lot except they were peace loving people of the 'leave us alone' kind.

Breer went out through the back door and looked towards Super Castle. It was now full of activity, the candlelight visible through all its windows often interrupted, so people must be moving about. He walked to the parental quarters and on ground level noticed through the woven screen door panels, shadowy figures on the porch. They were members of the guards, the two who had brought in Jaculo, joined by a high-ranking officer. They all started speaking at once, then the two juniors, realising their mistake, fell quiet to give the officer the privilege.

"Good to be able to speak with you, Breer," he started. "I have terrible news to convey, and terrible news for you and your family, but it will be particularly hard to give it to Baruta, which I will have to do eventually in any case, but maybe you can help me somewhat. I know it will be hard for you too, but Baruta was so proud of what was going to happen today."

Breer's throat tightened. For a moment he expected Officer Jari to tell him that Marquita had come off her horse and broken her neck or some such thing. He reacted almost in a whisper. "What is it, Jari, tell me."

"Marquita has escaped and must be now with Estabella in the Northland. I expect your father to take that very badly. I am very sorry, Breer, we tried to stop her, and would have easily done so but she had help from someone who burned the bridges for one thing. And also, what happened to Jaluco, you tell it," he said, nodding to one of his aides.

"When we carried him in and laid him down, he came to for a while, looking frightened saying, 'There was a very loud crack right in my face, Sniffer reared and threw me, never done such a thing before, a loud crack, very loud,' he said yesterday, but he cannot remember anything now, not even coming off his horse and he is so in the dumps about losing Swift. That's all, and then he was out of it again. He's back now, seems okay again, but can't remember a thing, we tried for him to repeat what happened to him and Swift. That horse was his claim to fame."

Breer had to use all his acting capabilities not to broadly grin when he heard of Marquita's successful escape. *Good on you, kid*, he thought. Jari would later report back that Breer had taken the terrible news rather well.

9
BARUTA 2

Jari hoped that Breer would make his unenviable task easier by preparing his father Baruta for the unexpected blow. But Breer felt unequal to the task. He would have to act like a thorough hypocrite to hide his delight at the turn of events, but at the same time he wanted to soften the task for Jari and to prepare Baruta for the coming blow. He was so pleased with the outcome, but at the same time he felt a large amount of sympathy for his dad, knowing full well what this would mean for him and the level of humiliation he now could experience. *There is only one person who can prepare Dad for this, and that is Mum*, he decided. She would also be very upset by the turn of events, but she would not be absolutely devastated. He had wondered a few times during previous weeks about Mum's fairly lacklustre reactions to Baruta's hyperbolic enthusiasm.

When he confronted Mum-Mariotte, he told her what had happened without displaying any emotion. Mariotte was sad and thoughtful. Looking at her son she remarked, "You are not at all sorry about it, are you?"

"No, Mum. Marquita was very unhappy about her fate. I felt for her. But I do feel sorry for Dad, he will take this very hard, he was so happy about her selection."

Coming down the stairs, Baruta noticed Jari standing a little apart from the others. The usually active and alert officer looked unhappy and nervous. Baruta had dressed up formally to face whatever he had to face. The thought that people might get some delight in bringing him bad news had strengthened his resolve to show no emotion. His worry was misplaced and for a brief moment Baruta forgot his own upset realising that Jari was dreading the moment he had to tell Baruta of Marquita's escape. As soon as he saw Baruta approaching, Jari straightened and greeted him stern faced with a formal military salute.

Baruta nodded. "You were given the task of giving me very bad news, Jari." Baruta felt deep sympathy for Jari, whom he had known since he was a small child, always full of promise and who had grown up into a brave and successful soldier.

"Yes, sir," Jari replied. "I am sad to report that Marquita has fled to the Northern lands."

"Tell me all you know, Jari," Baruta said in a gentle voice.

"When I left the unit to come here to see how Jaculo was, Marculas was still trying to catch up with Marquita, to bring her back, but the chances of him being successful must be small.

"Many strange things happened. Someone set fire to the two bridges, so to cross the river, Marculas and his men had to move a fair way back to where the river is shallow enough to ford it. It seems that when Jaculo had almost caught up with the Chosen One, his horse had a bad fall and had to be destroyed, while Jaculo landed on his head so badly that he only just has come to and can't remember anything that happened. He is still here in the recovery unit."

"Thank you, Jari. You and your men better have something to eat and drink, find Jansino, he will look after you. I have some things to attend to."

Baruta had taken the news extremely badly. He could not comprehend that his Marquita had done such a thing. The servants sympathised, and his wife seemed worried, but not at all enraged. He could not fathom it. And Breer acted absolutely strange. He had been so morose lately and now he acted as if he could not care less. From the reports coming in it was clear that she had been given help. His thoughts went straight to Janitis, that young fellow had been acting very strangely of late.

Now his whole life turned to ash. All his achievements turned from the heights he was on to foreseen new advancements into a heap of rubble. It might be best to resign from his position on the board before he was removed under some funny pretext.

Baruta went straight up to his study and closed the door. *Now it is only a matter of waiting till they will come and relieve me of most if not all of the duties that count.* He knew he could not go out on the street now and face up to people who either might laugh at him or be sorry for him as soon as they heard the news and news like this would travel fast, very fast.

Late that afternoon, Mariotte very much worried about Baruta's state of mind, came to keep him company for a while. She brought him the latest news gathered from Breer and Jansino who had made a brief visit to the main centre and from a few friends that had called in wanting to talk about the latest happening. From that it was clear that Marculas had followed Marquita right up to the Northlands gardens, but had been prevented by Estabella's men from taking her back. Estabella, apparently enraged by the unauthorised border crossing, had cut off the water supply to the Midlands gardens.

The Upper Host had been beyond reason, and released an edict declaring war on the north, mobilising the army and ordering them to immediately assemble in the southern gardens ready to invade the north. He also required all males, except those with valid exemptions, to register for military service. This order was obeyed, but very reluctantly.

Breer had plainly refused. "I take the consequences, whatever they are," he had said. There were a large number of people wandering about with 'NO WAR' notices pinned to their jackets.

Baruta secluded himself for the rest of the day.

Late morning of the day after, Jansino knocked on his door. "There is a High State carriage heading in this direction, sir. It looks important."

Baruta smiled and got up from his seat. "Thank you, Jansino." *Well, this is it*, he murmured to himself. *At least they are going to give me the bad news in style. I admire their good taste*, he thought with a grim smile. He stood ready on the front porch, when the carriage came to a stop, and with dignity he walked down the path, to meet whoever it was. It was Elderman Gentary, who was the oldest of the Elders and who extracted himself from the carriage with some difficulty. It amazed Baruta to see this older Elderman, whom he greatly liked, smiling up at him.

"Baruta, it saddens me that you had to suffer this." He extended his hand, something Elders seldom did. "It must be a severe blow to you, to have Marquita absconding. I convey not only my own sympathy but that of the whole government."

"Would you like to come in for a refreshment, your honour, and for a rest, after your journey?" Baruta asked.

"Yes please, and forget the 'your honour' bit for here and now."

"Thank you, sir," Baruta replied, while they moved inside. Jansino brought in fruit drinks and Gentary thanked him with a smiling nod. He sat there quietly for a few minutes.

"I am sure you have heard most of the disturbing news, Baruta. First Pontilious issued an edict to invade the Northlands gardens to repair the water supply that Estabella has turned off. To mobilise our forces and for all men to report for military duty forthwith. Our whole cavalry and most of our regular foot soldiers are now, as I speak, on the Midlands garden grounds, ready to invade the Northlands. A most worrying development.

"He did not consult the generals nor the Inner Six. An edict is an edict and must be obeyed. All the same there was a lot of criticism and Pontilious resigned from his position. The main reason was of course the humiliation of being rejected by the Chosen One.

"Capabilitis was unanimously elected to occupy the top job. He has scheduled a meeting in an hour's time from now, and he wishes you to be there as a representative of the people. If you can be ready in fifteen minutes or so, you can travel back with me in the chariot, tie your horse onto the back for your return."

"Thank you, Gentary, sir. I will just get my things and let my people know and then am ready to go."

Baruta found it hard to believe that instead of being stripped of his position, he was now travelling with the most senior Elder in a superior coach to join the Upper Host and the Elders, in what appeared to be a war council.

Gentary, in a soft voice, filled in the blanks in the happenings of the last days and the uncontrolled reaction of the then Upper Host, who appeared to have acted not in the interest of the nation, but motivated by his anger and perceived humiliation.

10
Janitis 2

He had Sniffer tied up some distance away, but not too far, obscured by trees. So far all had gone with textbook perfection. As soon as Marquita had passed the bridge, he would set it alight and return quickly home and into his bed, pretending that was where he had been all night. He felt assured of success. He heard the heavy thumping of Marquita's fast approaching horse, but then more and more the higher rhythm of another horse in pursuit, sounding lighter and fast. Sweat started to run down his face. No, this surely could not happen, so close to success, and then still to fail. But by now he was convinced that the pursuer was gaining. With trembling legs, he got up. Only one answer now, he had to throw Sniffer and himself in between Marquita and the rider chasing her. It might save Marquita. No matter what the cost was to Sniffer and himself. He hastened toward his horse. He heard a brief irregularity in the chasing horse's hoofbeats as if it had lost some ground, but soon it was beating out again with devastating regularity.

"Come on, Sniffer, we're in for it, the Almighty might bless us both." Mounting Sniffer and on the point of making his leap out of hiding, the air was pierced by a sequence of penetrating noises: a loud crack, as of a horse whip, followed by bone chilling sounds, a panicked shrieking, a crashing and a hard thud, then another less pronounced one. But the heavy hoofbeat of the obviously solid but slower horse continued. Who or what caused all this, he could only guess at. He dismounted and having secured Sniffer once more, hurried to his position under the bridge to light the fire. Marquita was closing in fast, while the distant sound of more horses in pursuit had stopped for a few minutes, increasing the fugitive's advantage. Then it started up again. Now he saw Marquita approach, the pale moonlight offsetting the heavy white horse, its rider just a hardly perceptible shadow on top. Both Janitis and Marquita were too intent on their actions to even try and glance at each other. Janitis was already lighting the fire, hearing and feeling the loud vibrating thumping of the horse hooves near his head.

The fire was slow to take. "Come on, come on." He lit a few little sticks from the slow burning centre, lit it in a different place, but it still would not take. He could hear the pursuing pack gaining ground. Have to try the north side of the bridge, not without Sniffer. More time lost by undoing Sniffer and riding him fast over the bridge to the north side. He did not worry now to be noticed, only one concern, to get the north side burning quickly. Once there he jumped off Sniffer, fell to the ground, half crawled half ran, getting under the bridge and setting light to it, remembering a little flask of oil in his back pocket taken for just that reason, sprinkled it on and shifted a little branch that was alight to it and then he saw the fire leap up. He heard Sniffer neigh in fear and move back. "Don't flee from me now, Sniffer," he moaned "and leave me stranded here." Just then the leader of the pack entered the bridge from the southern end, the fire still being insignificant there. It had to slow down a lot on the bridge's planking but was spurred on by his rider who noticed the flames leaping up at the northern end. The horse responded and leaped forwards just as the flames shot up high, reared, tossing his rider into the stream while backing off slowly.

The rest of the pack had now arrived including Marculas, some being busy fishing their man from the stream and trying to calm the scared horse. Janitis had scrambled away from the fire, trying to locate Sniffer, softly calling his name. He noticed with satisfaction the confusion on the south side. Then heard Marcula shouting, "Follow the river westward and we will ford it there."

Janitis smiled grimly. *You bastards you are still not giving up.* Having read up carefully and repeatedly on Estabella's escape, he knew exactly the route Marquita would take, it was the only route she could take to the cleft in the rock. The path up to that led through the garden lands up to pebble bar, where a narrow strip had been cleared of the boulders and pebbles to make it possible for people to communicate, just wide enough for one horse to pass through. It was seldom used, as

Midlanders were scared of the Northern people, because they held strange beliefs and were different. A few women had passed over and joined the Northies but no man was game enough to try and test the rumours which insisted that the Northlanders would castrate them. A few women from the North had passed over, mainly, it was believed, to pass on information to Estabella's cronies, but some had fallen in love with a Midlander and settled there, where they could have a man all for themselves while that was looked down upon by the country ruled and regulated by Estabella.

Janitis had never expected the guards to venture past the Midlanders' gardens onto the grounds north of pebble bar as, although not set out in hard and fast rules, conventionally the land north of pebble bar was considered Northlanders' territory. That border was seldom crossed except in cases when it was necessary to discuss an issue such as water supply. But as Marcula and his guards were now fording the river, they must have crossing that border in mind. It was unlikely they would catch Marquita before the pebble bar, so they must be planning to stop her on the long winding road before the cleft in the rock.

Sniffer had backed away far from the fire. It took Janitis more time than he had hoped for, but eventually he caught up with Sniffer and had to spend some time calming his horse. Then he was off as fast as he could manage towards the narrow breach in the pebble bar. It was impossible to cross the pebble bar on horseback, so they must be heading for the narrow path leading through. Janitis gave brief thought to the dangerous game they were playing. Estabella's forces were considerable and if she felt her territory had been invaded, she could make it very difficult for the middle ground people to cultivate their food supply.

Again, the race for time was on, but here Janitis had the advantage of travelling on the regular path, while the guards had to work their way back to the path after having forded the river further westwards. Arriving at 'the connect', as the pebble clearing was known, Janitis started by putting pebbles, medium to large ones, on the path but although somewhat effective he realised that with the large manpower they had they could clear the temporary blockage in little time. Then he wondered about the leaning tree hanging over the path. A large above ground root just looked as if this was the one that held up the tree. Surely without that one the tree would topple and fall over completely, blocking the entrance to the upper gardens.

Janitis grabbed over his shoulder unsheathing the sword, heavy and keen, and started with wide broad sweeps cutting across the thickness of the root. The sword bit easily into the fresh, green wood. Changing the direction of the cuts, he removed a wedge of juicy wood with each alternate cut. But as time went on speed became more essential. By now the sound of hooves again became a source of concern. Why didn't that bloody tree fall, that root just had to be essential for it staying upright. In utter desperation Janitis tied the rope that lay coiled over the saddle's pummel and, looping one end around Sniffer's neck, tied the other high up on the tree trunk and urged Sniffer to pull. Sniffer obliged with all his might, but the tree would not move, while the sound of approaching hooves hitting the surface became more and more pronounced. Their repetitive rhythmic quality was an inducement to Janitis's attack on the second root. Without realising it, he was hitting in time with the sound coming from the pack getting nearer. At the same time the sound of Janitis's blade hitting the root acted like the action of a whip on Sniffer's back. The moonlight now painted an eerie dancing picture on the heads and riders of the approaching group of horses.

Then it happened. A crunching reverberating crack tore through the air and all at once the tree toppled, in an unexpected, strange twisting way down to block the path. One major branch turned on a swing path in Sniffer's direction and because of the shortness of the rope, Sniffer could not escape the branch that with increasing speed crushed Sniffer's back. The harder he tried to escape, the more he brought down the branch on his back, breaking him into a helpless victim of his own strength.

Janitis's jubilation turned into instant despair, seeing his beloved horse being ruined. "Sniffer," he cried. Seeing the unsavable animal's agony, he raised his sword and brought it in desperate anger hard down on the horse's neck cutting across major blood vessels. Then he scrambled, crying, over the pebble border along the northern edge to conceal himself as much as possible from the approaching guards and working himself in the direction west for an unknown destination.

11
Marquita 2

Marquita relaxed as soon as she passed into the Northlands gardens. Here she felt safe, as Midlanders respected the sovereignty of the north over the Northlands gardens. There was not an official or even semi-official agreement to that. Convention dictated that the Northlands gardens were the property of the north, and the southern gardens belonged to the Midlanders. If there was a reason to cross that agreed border, one would draw the attention of one of Estabella's subjects and state the reason, ask whether it was okay to do so.

Marquita sighed and stopped pressuring Fearless who slowed down to an easy walk. In the distance she could see the momentous rock wall stretching out, but it still was too far to discern the cleft in the wall where she would need to pass through to enter Estabella's domain. How she looked forward to that, after her recent adventure and her escape from a public deflowering by that old man. Then her thoughts focussed on Janitis, without whose support it would have been impossible to escape the guardsmen on their fast horses. At one time she had almost been caught, but something unexpected had happened and her pursuer had come down in a violent crash, but why?

The path before her was long and wound its way between large rocks and boulders dotting the landscape. In between were flat irregularly shaped bits of ground, well cultivated, where the Northlanders grew their food, and larger areas covered with grass where horses and small cows were grazing. The path was smooth enough, working its way up to the foot of the rock wall the slow way. Here and there it twisted, doubling down on itself. The moonlight reflected in places from the smooth rock face and then, hidden from sight, she noticed a vertical dark break. That was it, the cleft in the wall. She patted her mount. "Almost there, Fearless," she laughed, "almost there, well done."

Raising her head she noticed a familiar sound, it was that of a pack of horses travelling as fast as this terrain would allow them. My God, no, no she never had thought this remotely possible, chasing after her on Northland property, would they stop at nothing? She heard that they moved with considerable speed and she urged Fearless on to hurry up. The cleft in the wall was still, as the path went, at least one hundred metres away or more, and all at once the horse's footfalls sounded too close for comfort. She pleaded with her mount to go faster. It was tired by now and reluctantly began to canter. She could see the cleft nearing; but at the same time her pursuers were catching up. Oh no, not this, so close to success and still failing. Again, it seemed hopeless. She could see how close she was, but they were going to catch her in the next twenty metres or so.

From her left like a ribbon of grey, a band of riders two by two came in a broad arch, circling between her and the riders chasing her, who came to an abrupt stop, seeing their way blocked. The band of riders rode small lean horses. Estabella's men, for that was who they were, riding two by two, all holding the reins in their left hand and a solid stick in the other, keeping it aimed at the guards, who unsheathed their swords. Marculas knew that if he would try to attack, he could unleash something so bad he might very well regret it for the rest of his life.

"Hand her over, she is ours," he yelled.

"That's for Estabella to decide," came the answer.

"She's ours, a Midlands girl, you have no right to hold her."

"You have no right to be here uninvited, you are on Northern territory, we want you to leave now."

A new mount was brought out for Marquita, she was helped to dismount. Marquita petted Fearless and thanked him for helping her to reach safety. Her replacement mount was a lean bay horse. One of Estabella's men took Fearless by the reins and walked over to Marculas's party, looking with disdain at their unsheathed swords, stopping just in front of Marculas. "Your horse," he said, then turned his back and walked away.

Marculas turned and spoke briefly to his men, they then sheathed their swords, turned and left the way they came. Marquita and her entourage moved forward into the outer opening to the cleft.

Once inside Marquita was surprised to find herself in a more or less circular hall, open to the sky. From the outside it had appeared as a cleft in the rock but inside it was spacious and lit up with many flares. Her escort treated her with kind respect, asked if she needed to rest for a while or if she wanted to carry on their way inside the rock.

"I would so much wish to meet Estabella," she replied.

"You will very soon," she was told. One by one the riders took a flare, lit it by holding it against one of the flares spread around the area, then rode into the cleft, first one of the men, then another one, then Marquita was motioned to move in, the rest following one by one in a single file. The long thread-like band of riders wound itself through the long narrow gorge sufficiently well-lit by the flares. Apart from the sound of the hooves on the stone path it was quiet and comfortable to travel, Marquita no longer living in fear of being caught before reaching her destination.

12
Estabella's Northland

Rock walls rose steeply on both sides fusing somewhere high up. Marquita was fascinated by the eerie moving patterns painted by the flares on the stone walls as they moved along. She had expected that the cleft would quickly lead to some kind of open space, but travelling through this narrow space hemmed in on both sides by solid rock seemed to go on forever. Apart from the horses' footfalls there was no sound at all, almost spookily quiet. Marquita could still not relax, being full of anticipation of what would happen next. Eventually the gorge widened bit by bit then unexpectedly opened up widely giving straight ahead a view of open green landscape dotted with settlements. To the right there was a very large cave. The outside landscape, lit by the full moon and dotted by settlements, looked enticing and romantic to her. The moonlight could not illuminate the cave, but this was taken care of by a multitude of flares standing about. They all dismounted.

A figure in a floor length gown dissolved out of the shadowy background. "Welcome, Marquita."

"How do you know my name?"

"We make it our business to know many things, and are very happy that you came to us. But first come with me to your temporary accommodation, for you to refresh and have a rest.

"My name is Symphonia One, my younger sister Symphonia Two, the next one Symphonia Three. My mother is very musical but lacked imagination when it came to name giving." Symphonia laughed a clear laugh sounding like a little bell. "But come with me, you can freshen up and get some sleep."

"Freshening up is good, but sleeping is the last thing on my mind, I want to talk and meet people, especially I would so much like to see Estabella."

"And Estabella would love to see you too. Come, have a wash and a drink and then we will go and see her. I had thought that you would need to rest first, that's why I prepared this room for you, but if you are too excited to sleep, then just have a wash and a drink and we will go and see the chief."

Ten minutes later they were on their way.

"It's only a brief walk, Estabella's quarters are close by."

Through a doorway, the solid looking double doors wide open, they came into what looked like a meeting hall with large windows looking out at the village bathed in transparent moonlight. Then through another doorway into a smaller room, with a large table in the centre, the table being a fixture chiselled out of the rock. So most of this cave must have been manmade,

Marquita decided, the result of many years of hard work. A dozen or so chairs were arranged around the table. "This is her cabinet room, where she meets with ministers and advisors," Symphonia volunteered.

There was another open door at the end where a woman sat looking at papers by candlelight, looking up as Symphonia and Marquita approached. "Ah, you brought her straight in, Symphy One," she laughed. "Esty will be so pleased."

"Great, Sjasta."

The woman addressed as Sjasta knocked on the door behind her, then opened it almost immediately. Marquita had not heard anything from the inside and Sjasta, in a loud singsong voice, announced, looking inside, "Esty, she's here, the girl that escaped," then nodded with her head to indicate to Marquita to go in.

Marquita took a sharp astonished breath when she saw a very old, elegant lady approach her. It seemed like an apparition to her, this tall figure in a long velvety floor length gown, face lined with age, floating up to her. Estabella laughed, seeing the look of bewilderment on Marquita's face.

"Come in, my child," she said, opening her arms wide. "I am so pleased that you feel well enough after your escape to see me straight away. I have been looking forward to this since I found out you made a run for it, which is not very long ago." She laughed again. "You look as if you saw a ghost when you walked in, what had you expected, that I would look like the

Estabella pictures in the history books? Those drawings and imaginations are based on how I might have looked fifty years ago and in fantasy. I have grown old in the meantime."

"Oh, yes, no, sorry," stammered Marquita blushing. "What shall I call you, madam?"

"Not madam, that's for sure."

"Sorry."

"Enough sorrys for now, just call me Estabella, that is my name after all, and that has been what you have been calling me if you talked about me before you met me, right?"

"Yes, madam, eh Estabella, I mean."

"Now, let's sit down. We have a lot to talk about, you and I. Sjasta, would you bring us some sweet juice, please."

"Sure, won't be long."

"Now, tell me all about it," Estabella smiled.

"I decided to imitate your escape, so I managed when I was still at home to get permission to go to the library and borrow books and read up on whatever I could find on your escape, then try to do the same."

"But first, things were not the same for you as they were for me," Estabella interrupted," and those written accounts are largely fiction. You were at the castle for five nights, I only for two. In between the two nights, I, or I should say my body, was being cleaned and anointed for the sacrifice. And of course they fed me drugs and alcohol, but unlike all of those that went before me, I managed partly by good luck and partly because of the incompetence of my keepers to ditch almost all of that. When you get enough of the stuff into you, you are completely in their hands. But, I interrupted, please carry on."

"Well, anyway I believed what I read, and most or almost all went as planned. Twice they caught up with me, and twice I thought I had lost. I do not know what happened when the fastest of the guards caught up with me. I threw my scarf in his face, and that made him fall back a little, but then when he was only a horse length behind me, I heard a crack and then a lot off crashing and he must have fallen. Why I still don't understand."

"You had some help, didn't you? Somebody burnt down the bridges."

"Yes, Janitis, without his help I could not have succeeded. But he would have been at the bridge, to burn it as soon as I crossed it, so the rest could not follow me."

"He might have tripped up your pursuer, then rode or ran to the bridge, by that time you would have been over and he set fire to it. Possible, yes?"

"He would have needed to be very fast, I find it somehow difficult to imagine he managed to do all that. The second time was when your men intervened, they almost had me then."

"My people were watching as soon as you crossed into our garden lands. Nobody expected the guards to follow. They would have fought the guards if they had tried to take you once you were on our grounds. They let you go, thinking you would make it on your own, but once it became unlikely you could do that they intervened. The guards made a stupid mistake which the Midlanders will sorely regret. There must be pay-off for invading our territory, this cannot go unpunished."

"Will you go to war with the Midlands?" Marquita inquired worriedly.

"No, war is not a consideration. We have other ways, they will find out tomorrow. Even now the connecting path is being blocked completely, and a sign put up that anyone trying to cross will be killed. Then, we have excess of water here and a long-standing arrangement that we supply the water for their gardens. That stream also will be blocked during the night. They can still water their gardens from the river, but it means carrying it uphill. Hard and tedious work. That's all. I am waiting for their response. They need us, we can carry on very well without them. Not that I prefer it this way, but I want apologies and a significant payment of damages. I'm sure they will ask for discussions, but I will be very severe with them."

"When I was detained at the castle I had this lovely companion sister, Ariotto, looking after me. She carried the keys to the exit door and the medicine cupboard where the drug was kept to make me passive and compliant. I could deceive this naive woman all the way along. I felt good and bad about it at the same time. She had a weakness for alcohol which I could use to my full benefit." Marquita started to laugh. "It was funny and awful at the same time, she was like putty in my hands. Not the slightest idea she was being manipulated all the way along. But I had to escape, and escape I did, thanks to the help of Janitis and your good soldiers."

Next day Marquita was up early. She washed and dressed, being as quiet as she could so as not to wake Symphy One, who was looking after Marquita till she was used to the ways of Northland. The temperature was moderate inside her rocky room. She had already noticed that rock dwellers had their living and dining rooms at the outside of the rock face, with large windows looking out at the landscape ahead. It sloped down from the rock face for a long distance, to rise again further away, with big mountains in the far distance. Close by the landscape was dotted with small cosy looking dwellings, mostly built out of blue stone pieces which came from the mountain where the rock dwellers had enlarged their caves, or excavated new places to live by chipping away at the hard stone. All the chips and pieces were discarded down the rock face, where they were then collected by 'outsiders' to build their residences under and in between trees, or on the open meadows.

Some of the roofs were made out of plant materials, leaves and branches, others were covered by flat pieces of blue stone. Very few had used handmade clay fired tiles. Marquita enjoyed the picturesque look of it all.

The morning was cool and fresh, the sky cloudless. Walking in between the houses, looking up at the rock face, she could now see the extent to which the rock was inhabited. From where she had emerged from the long narrow passage, after entering the cleft, the rock face extended in both directions as far as the main river to the left and butting into a massive mountain range to the right. The rock face showed signs of occupation at many levels. It would require lots of stairways inside. In between the windows and above and below were a large number of smaller holes, Marquita assumed for ventilation, or light channels for rooms not facing the outside, or chimneys for kitchens. Remarkable.

Returning she found Symphony One awake, and a young man cooking breakfast on a stove using a wood fire in an alcove. The stove was installed against the back wall of the room. Marquita had not noticed it at first, but now the smell of roasting meat and vegetables had drawn her attention to it. The smoke was rising up into a round hole in the ceiling overhung by a stone extension.

"Estabella wants to see you after lunch," Symphony One announced. "She seems eager to talk some more with you. Make use of it while you can, she is very busy at times. She also has times that she gets very tired and needs to sleep a lot."

"Sit down here." Estabella gestured at a chair facing the view over the estate. "Isn't it wonderful," she added.

"Yes, indeed. I went for an early walk this morning, enjoyed it very much. The houses look so beautiful there, no fences, just naturally as if nature had grown them. And I like the colour of the stacked stone walls. And then this rock; walking down there and looking up you can really appreciate how many people must be living here. And what passages for air and smoke ventilations as well as stairways are carved inside, what a job it must have been."

"And still is," Estabella added, "this is an ongoing affair, a continual construction. Well planned. I made sure of that and still do. But I am old now and someone has to take over soon. It is never easy to hand over the reins. When I arrived here everything was all so disorganised, nothing was planned, they just did a bit, everybody did things his own way. I say 'his' on purpose, it was the men then who controlled everything, or did not control it is more correct. It was one God Almighty great shemozzle.

"When I arrived, I had a very good start. They admired me as if I were supernatural, returned from the dead instead of having escaped it. Then I have this natural way of being able to organise matters, to make order out of chaos. I started in small ways, but they all saw I had talent, and I am very proud of what I have achieved here, and now of course it will be difficult to let go. Somebody younger will need to take over, but it has to be someone with courage and talent, because our system here is unique and even small changes could have big effects. I don't want my work to be destroyed. I am talking a lot, aren't I."

"It is so nice and relaxing to have you talking to me in my own language. I know that the Northern tongue is not all that different from Midlandish, but I have to concentrate very hard to understand and even then, I miss some."

"Well, I will explain all to you, our system, how it works. Took me years to achieve what I wanted to achieve, and most of my subjects are happy and accept the system as it operates now, but that does not mean that all agree. What was very obvious was that the men made a hash of things. When here and there, now and then things worked well, it always meant that they were run by the bigwig's offsider, his helper, second in charge, assistant, secretary, whatever, always a woman of course, doing the work, the thinking. When a man assisted a man, you ended up with a mess, not twice as big, but mess squared. So I saw it as my task to try and motivate the men to do something different and let the women just get on organising the show.

"You can imagine how carefully I had to tread, not to step on toes, so to speak. You must realise, of course in the early days I had no official standing, no power to do anything. Going for power would have made me suspect straight away. I had to move in small ways at first, get results and then later on maybe use a bit of muscle to move things forward. Oh, it has been such a satisfying journey. I planted seeds for new ideas carefully in people's minds. Often, they forgot that I had suggested it and thought it was all their own idea, and came up to me suggesting what I had sown months earlier in a vague manner so they could work on it and then were proud of their own cleverness. Never worry about the glory, the result is all that matters. But what about you, I should let you talk a bit. Because I am so glad you are here. If you like it here, and I think you will, you can become a very valuable contributor to our community, of that, I am sure."

"I too am very happy to be here now and to feel safe. But I am bound to my love: Janitis. We have agreed to meet at a certain place just south of the Midlands, where we both as kids used to hang out a lot, and to get married."

Estabella's face darkened for a moment.

"Ah, getting married, it's not the best thing to do. The weak get married because they need a constant companion. But you are strong, you have proven as much. You deceived Ariotto, even though you were fond of her, but you had to do that because your aims were more important than Ariotto's happiness and ultimate comfort. You did what you needed to do and now here we are, discussing matters of principle in a most pleasant environment. If you had failed, you would by now be the wife of an old man you don't respect. *You are strong*. We both are strong, Marquita," she added softly. "You and I are very much alike, you and I have a lot in common. You will follow your destiny, like I followed mine, and even if now you feel obliged to follow your childish love affair and honour your pledge to Janitis, one day you will look for a different bigger destiny. You are not cut out just to be a wife and mum, you are bigger than that. Mark my words.

"I have told you only a miniscule amount of what I want to tell you. But now I need a brief rest before I meet with my inner circle. In the meantime, let me tell you, your presence gives me great happiness. I hope you stay with us for a long time, but I will in no way stand in the way of you achieving your aims. I will assist you instead. But before you leave, I want you to fully understand what I have done here and why. I hope to talk with you again tomorrow."

But that was not what happened. From here on Estabella was more than ever busy with matters of state. Her spies had already informed her that the Midlanders were mobilising their army. All men capable of serving had to report to their local recruitment centre. The southern gardens between the river and pebble border were teeming with armed midland horsemen. What was up, what did they have in mind?

The Northland had to respond, for fear that otherwise the Midlanders would breach pebble border again to re-establish their water supply. She could not allow that to happen.

"The gall of them, we are the abused party, they breached our borders, we want an apology and appropriate recompense."

Soon armed horsemen were streaming out of the cleft. It was an impressive sight to see them emerging from the cleft in the rock as if performing a drill, streams of horsemen two abreast milling through the fields, which were days ago the workplace for peaceful farming and horticulture.

A high-level Midland army general, wearing his accoutrements to made him very distinctive, rode ahead of a phalanx of Midland horsemen. Instead of the usual fighting dress he wore his ceremonial uniform with a plumed hat, making him very visible. An arrow arising from the Northern side flew in a wide arch in the general's direction and ended up in the soil two metres ahead of his mount. A rolled-up parchment was attached to its shaft. A lieutenant retrieved it and handed it to the general. It was addressed to the Midland government. The general handed it back to the lieutenant with instructions, who rode off in a gallop to ford the river and deliver it to the head of state, which was of course the new Upper Host, appointed following the resignation of the then head of state after celebration day.

13
Deliberations

To the head of state of the Midlands
  Dear sir,
  I write to you in response to a baffling and disturbing mobilisation of your forces and their employment in large and threatening numbers on the garden area between the river and pebble border which Midlanders habitually cultivate. Because of this threatening display of forces I have found it prudent to respond in kind, and have a significant force positioned north of the pebble strip. As your forces in a small number have on full moon night found it necessary to breach the pebble border and at full speed invade our territory without permission, I have found it necessary to block your water supply until such a time that I receive an acceptable apology and recompense for this intrusion.
  At the time I assumed the action was the result of a misguided local officer-in-charge who went far beyond his level of rank and

responsibility in your power structure and would be disciplined for his action. From what happened subsequently I must be totally mistaken. The escalation of threatening display means that we must now prepare for the possibility of a repeat of what happened on full moon night on a massive scale. Such an action would be foolish and lead to armed conflict, which I, and I hope you, would like to prevent.

After the territorial disputes and physical fights between our two countries many decades ago, which were never concluded with a formal settlement, we have nevertheless lived in peace and some cooperation, accepting the pebble strip as a border line between both your and our level of influence and administration along those lines.

I am therefore deeply disturbed by recent developments, which if continued can only lead to war, at great expense and suffering to both nations. I therefore demand no further escalation of these actions. If you do increase your pressure, it will in little time lead to an armed conflict. Do not count on an easy victory. We will defend at all cost our customary rights above pebble border.

It would be advisory to send an emissary to talk this over soon. Talking is better than fighting. But be assured with the threat you pose to us now, I will not and never will restore your water supply, and an apology for moonlit night's invasion is mandatory.

On behalf of Northlands inhabitants and interest,

ESTABELLA.

Capabilitis had been the Upper Host for only a few days when this epistle was delivered to him. He was saddled with the unwise emotional decision taken by the previous Upper Host before he resigned. His decision was clearly motivated by vindictive feelings resulting from his humiliation when the Chosen One had preferred taking extreme risky action by escaping rather than being honoured as the Superior bride. When on the morning of the celebration consummation, his bride had escaped and the Northland cut off the water supply to Midlands' garden lands, he had flown into a Superior rage and declared renewal of the war against Northland. This declaration was not made to Northland, but to the Inner Six and his generals.

"Immediate mobilisation, building of much bigger bridges over the river and sending a large force north of the river, attacking and recovering all the lands up to the cleft." It had been received by one and all with little enthusiasm, but the order of the Supreme commander was to be followed at all cost.

Capabilitis had no taste for a war, which could only lead to a lot of disturbance, loss of income and many benefits, and above all loss of life. He was also well aware of the last time Midlanders had tried to win back the area between the pebble strip and the rock. At first it had seemed that they were going to take it easily, but then the Northlanders had fought back with much determination and with complete disregard for personal safety and in a degrading bloody battle had pushed the Midlanders against the pebble strip and over it on foot, because the horses couldn't handle that terrain. The outcry after had been: 'No more war, no more war ever again'.

Now here he was confronted with this document, which he was sure clearly defined the future if he would continue his predecessor's edict. Not to do so, had also grave consequences for the dignity of the office. If he would not deliver on Pontilious's edict, why should his subjects deliver on his future edicts. It would without doubt dilute his own power. An edict was an edict. It was of course a consideration that Pontilious had acted both in anger and without consultation with either the Inner Six or any of his generals. A very sticky situation.

Estabella asked for consultation but the edict left no room for negotiations. On the other hand, the consequences of continuing along the path demanded by Pontilious would be so destructive and lead to enormous ruination. Giving in to Estabella's demands would be a slap in the face for Pontilious and degrading for the nation.

He sighed, he had not expected that if he ever came to office, he would be faced with something this difficult and disheartening. One thing he had to do straight away, was to give an order to the military not to escalate their actions, and not at all breach the pebble border or make any incursions on Northland territory without further orders. Then he ordered a meeting of the Inner Six.

The round table accommodated ten people, six members, only five present now. One of the positions was vacant as Capabilitis now filled the Upper Host's chair, which was separate in a raised enclosed seat overlooking the table. To his left were two occupied seats, the third empty one representing the vacancy caused by Pontilious's resignation and the resulting upgrading of Capabilitis to the Supreme position. On his right were three occupied chairs. Of the remaining four seats completing the circle, three chairs were now taken by two generals and Baruta representing the people, one chair left vacant.

Capabilitis read the edict of his predecessor, waited a few minutes, giving the members a chance to reread it from a copy they all had in front of them. Then he read out Estabella's letter.

"I will not deliberate on the difficulty we are facing but leave it now for you to discuss and guide me into the best action to take. Whatever action we take will have grave consequences."

The chairman, sitting to Capabilitis's right, opened the discussion, which was lively and presented different and opposing views, from a right out attack to winning back the once lost higher ground, to appeasement and negotiation. The generals, on questioning, were very upbeat about an easy win and regaining the upper gardens for the Midlands. Then they were confronted with the last Midland—Northland war, when at first victory seemed assured, but then the Northland, from high positions, bodies well protected by rocky outcrops, managed with fast arrows to pick off Midlanders one by one, followed up with a fast cavalry attack driving the panicking Midlanders down towards the pebble strip where they were bloodily defeated. They were left without an answer when asked if the same could not happen again.

The chairman gave Baruta the opportunity to give his views.

"Not my views, your excellencies, I represent the views of the people. The people have very little taste for war. Able men have obeyed the edict and registered for service, but without enthusiasm. Of the others, not compelled to enlist, many now go around with 'No War' rosettes on their clothes. Many feel that war with the Northland would serve no good purpose and would like to go back to where things were before all this happened."

"What is your personal opinion, Baruta?" came the voice of the Supreme One.

"My opinion is the same as that of the people, your honour. It would be an absolute disaster to go to war with the Northland people, for them, but even more so for us."

"Why do you say that?" one of the elders asked.

"Because it would unite them in their purpose, but it would divide us between ourselves, your honour."

It was silent for a moment. Then the voice of the Supreme One announced loud and clear, "My edict, which is at odds with the edict of Pontilious, is that war must be avoided if possible. That's an edict. I appoint Baruta as our representative to the Northland, to extract the best possible outcome that can avoid war without causing catastrophic humiliation for our side."

"I am honoured, your excellency, with the trust you show in me. But the missive of Estabella leaves me little room for negotiation. She will require an apology. But of course, I will do my utmost to avoid humiliation."

"Do the best you can," was the Upper Host's instruction.

14
Envoy

They met him at the border with a six-horse escort carrying purple and yellow banners, the colours of the Midlands. He was saluted in military fashion and respectfully guided to the cleft. Baruta made use of the opportunity to familiarise himself with the lay of the land, its strategic significance and especially when passing through the cleft and entering the hall behind it, he could see firsthand the enormous defensive capabilities inherent in this largely natural phenomenon. Looking up, he saw a large part of the walkways built for the soldiers to stand on and fire over the stone parapet, used with such devastating effect in the last armed conflict and causing such disastrous losses to the Midland army, were still largely intact.

He was offered a drink of water, politely declined, and then they proceeded in single file though the gorge. At long last they entered the open area and straight away moved to Estabella's quarters. Seeing her approaching him from some twenty metres or so away, he held his breath for a moment, being overcome by her powerful royal bearing. She seemed to be floating rather than walking in his direction. With an easy smile, she stopped a short distance away, bowed her head. "Welcome, envoy from the Midlands," she said.

"Pleased to be here," Baruta replied, also bowing. "Please tell me how I should address you."

Estabella involuntarily burst out laughing, then checked herself, noticing Baruta's confusion. "So daughter, so father," she said. "They were the first words Marquita said when we met. Call me Estabella, that is my name, and if I may call you Baruta then we can concentrate on the substance that really matters. But before we sit down to talk is there anything you need?"

"No, thanks," he replied.

They sat down in the meeting room, which gave their meeting a formal atmosphere.

"I have, and I hope you agree, not invited any aide-de-camps, and I notice that you came by yourself. I have also on purpose made no arrangements for our talks to be recorded by a clerk, so we can talk freely and candidly without having to be overcareful with our utterances."

"Suits me. I have of course read your message to our government, and it seems to leave not much room for negotiation. Let me assure you, Estabella, that we want to avoid war for a start."

"I also have no desire to go to war with the Midlands, or with anybody for that matter," she added, "but the presence of your forces in such a large number across the pebble border has left us wondering about your intention. Your Superior ruler's edict is ordering war, if I'm not wrong."

"By now there has been a new edict from His Honour Capabilitis, contradicting the edict from his predecessor."

"An edict can be overruled, I thought that impossible."

"It has never been done before, this is the first time."

They were silent for a moment, then Estabella started. "We are not here to exchange blows with each other, but to bring the situation back to normal. What I demanded in my message to your government, seems to me perfectly reasonable. I cannot and will not negotiate with a knife to my throat. When I turned off the water it was to let you know that what had happened was inexcusable and makes us feel vulnerable.

"But I assumed that the invasion was the action of some overzealous commander, who would be reprimanded for his actions. I expected some mea culpa and apology. Instead, we were faced with an escalation, which makes us fear that your intention is a further invasion, possibly to turn the water back on, or to try and capture our garden lands. It should not amaze you that we will not allow this. And even if you were to take our garden lands, you can never get through the gorge, you realise. You should also be aware that the stream runs in part through an opening in the rock. We would be in a position to poison the water, which would poison the land. What use is that to anybody. I do not want war, all the devastation of land and loss of life, all I want is a reasonable response, an apology, some recompense and of course the withdrawal of your troops."

"Estabella, I fully understand you are aggrieved. But I have to come back with something that will make it possible to retreat with some sort of dignity. You might feel this is too much to ask, but neither you nor I want escalation. So let us try as hard as we can to reverse the situation and get back to where we were before all this started."

"Let's have some juice and something to eat," Estabella suggested and called out for Sjasta. Food and drink were brought in. They ate quietly for a while.

"Your daughter is very happy here," Estabella started after a while. "All the same I'm sorry to say that we will not keep her, I'm sure of that. She has different plans and her own purpose. She would have been a valuable asset to our community but seems to be determined to attach herself to a young man called Janitis."

"Ah, Marquita. Janitis. Yes, what a pity. She should have been a man then..." he stopped himself in mid-sentence, realising his blunder. "Well, of course, I speak of the Midland priorities."

"A woman is good for marrying and supportive duties, ha, ha," replied Estabella.

"Janitis, he is not here, I believe."

"No, I have absolutely no idea where he is and if he is all right, but Marquita appears to believe that she will be able to find him. I have because of the recent developments had little chance to spend much time with her. I assume you would like to talk with her."

"Better not on this occasion," Baruta replied.

"Can I tell her you were here to negotiate for the Midlanders, it will greatly ease her mind. One of her concerns is that by escaping she might have ruined your career."

Baruta thought for a moment, smiled. "Yes, that will be all right."

"Now, back to business. I am sure you have worked out some position that you hope will be acceptable to me, and you can sell at your end."

Baruta smiled, being surprised with her direct approach. "Yes, you are right. I weighed the possibilities, and I do realise there is little wiggle room, but the situation is too serious for me not to try. Let's start with the easy bit. We could withdraw half of our troops, you could follow and do the same, continue this until just a few remain on both sides. Now for the more difficult bit. Rather than using water supply as a weapon, allow it to flow, on the understanding that a substantial apology will be forthcoming very soon. This might give me enough to soften the insecurity and antagonism that may be felt on our side. We can garden without your water supply by bringing it up from the river, but it would make it hard for us, at least in the immediate future.

"Compensation. Would a goodwill gesture not suffice? Like a breeding couple of excellent horses instead of a major payback, which would be seen as a humiliation."

Estabella looked thoughtful. "One thing we want and now need more than anything. This incident and particularly the follow up of mobilisation and threatening action has affected our feelings of security. I want a secure border, that cannot be violated. Without a formal border agreement, we have so far satisfactorily coexisted for decades. What has happened now has changed things from our perspective. I want guarantees that we don't have to be on our guard all the time for your more aggressive elements to try and take from us what is ours.

She continued, "We, for a very long time, owned all the land down to the river; you, for a very short time, possessed all the land up to the rock; and we drove you back to the pebble strip. We have lived with this situation for many decades. Now I need security. That is essential."

"Something good could come out of this. If we could formalise the situation that could lead to a peace agreement and a firm border determination," Baruta responded.

"Let the centre of the pebble ridge be the border," Estabella agreed.

"Would you consider to proceed along those lines," said Baruta. "Of course, you realise that I can only advise, the Upper Host decides on the advice of the Inner Six, but if you decide to agree in principle, I will do my utmost to convince my superiors that this is the best and safest way to go."

Estabella then called in Sjasta to prepare a memorandum of understanding.

15
Estabella explains

"Marquita, at last we have a chance to talk. You had a look around and talked with people, I assume, while I was busy with matters of state. It will make it easier for me to tell you how things work up here, if you have not yet worked it out for yourself. I had a very capable and approachable Midland envoy here, trying his best to reach some kind of settlement. We might have succeeded, but he could not decide, the decision rests with the Super-whatever on advice of the elevated six." Estabella said mockingly. "For a man he was very good, excellent as a matter of fact."

"And he did not want to see me?" Marquita said, "I'm disappointed, or wouldn't you let him?"

"Ah, you found out, you clever girl."

"I saw him being escorted in from a long distance, and it looked like him on horseback, never really a comfortable horseman, but I wasn't a hundred percent sure."

"Yes, it was him, so you can rest assured that his status has not been deteriorated by your escape. And no, he did not want to talk with you now. 'This is not the occasion,' he said. But you are much like each other as far as I can ascertain. Pity he is male, ha, ha. He wanted to know if Janitis was here, he would rather see you abandoning the boy. So would I. But I already realise that if you set your mind on something, you will not easily abandon it. In that respect you and I and your dad are alike.

"But what have you found out? That we do not castrate most men, yes? We just give young men or boys, if they don't show any promise by the age of ten, 'never-never' herb to eat, which makes them infertile. Everything functions all right, but no productive outcome. Some of our clever chaps researching herbs and tabulating what people ate, mostly in the outlying areas where there is a lot of harvesting of what is found growing wild, found a correlation between a certain herb, which is a tasty vegetable, being eaten regularly by men, and the absence of offspring. It was really not so clever at all, because colloquially it is called 'never-never' just for that reason. Common folks called it that because they noticed men who favoured that green, seldom fathered children. So that's a good way to keep our genetic material good and healthy. A bit of selective breeding if you like, as we do with pets and livestock. This was not the first development I got going, but easily the hardest one, and easily the one that could be soon disbanded if I hand over the reins to the wrong person.

"So, our children are all fathered by talented men. Whether it be in art, science, whatever. But we don't want to get them involved with organisational matters. When I came here, men were in charge of just about everything, but I soon noticed that when they had a woman as an assistant, which they often did, and they let the assistant look after things, it all functioned better. So, bit by bit I got men focussing on other matters and managed to get women to look after organisation. It has worked like a charm. It was not easy. It has taken time.

"We discourage our fertile men from marrying. Let them spread their seed far and wide, ha, ha. Especially among our more talented women, that way we will end up with a cleverer next generation. Each generation should be superior to the previous one. Quite a number of the infertile men choose to marry, even though they can't have any children. And of course it takes two to tango. There seem to be a lot of women who prefer it that way too, to have a man all to themselves. At first, I tried to stop marriage all together, but soon realised that it would not work, and then decided it does not really matter in any case.

"So here we are. The talented men are encouraged to educate themselves or pursue any field where their talent and interest takes them, and in this way they contribute to our community. I have a vision and I try to realise it with all my strength.

"You can call me a dictator if you like; I take advice from a group of close aides, not that different from your system, but by the Midlanders' system it's a man who takes the decisions aided by male assistants, here it is me helped by females. I think this works better by far. My control and influence with the rock dwellers is absolute or nearly so, and the lands adjoining are also under my very close control, sticking with my rules and ideas, but the areas very far removed from here are mainly inhabited by free dwellers. They do very much as they please. I don't worry too much about them. Some want to escape from my authority and do so by moving out far enough away from here, so I cannot direct or influence them. But I do want my experiment to continue, even if it is only at the rock and the adjoining lands. I need someone similarly inspired to take over from me. So when I heard about you and saw your strength I had some hopes." Estabella smiled at Marquita.

"No, I am not the one you need. For one I am absolutely tied to Janitis and I want him all for my own. I also want his children. I just may become your average boring housewife."

"But not forever, I am sure, you've got more to contribute," Estabella replied.

16
History

"The difference between me and the ones that went before me and suffered that awful end of their young lives, is that I was not going to let it happen," Estabella started off with, "same decision as you made. But the history of my escape has been romanticised. For one, I don't know how the ones that went before me felt about the so-called honour to be slaughtered on the sacrificial altar, maybe they were not aware of what was going to happen to them. But I was, and I wanted to live and would do whatever it took to escape my promised fate.

"I was also smart enough to realise that from the onset they were going to make me submissive by giving me drugs to deaden all the normal fear and reactions. Same as you, I had to deceive my carer and companion. Fortunately, she was dumb and naive, again same as in your case, and I also managed to mislead her and avoided drinking the potions to deaden my feelings. So far, all the same.

"But my escape was much simpler than yours. There were very few guards and they were all celebrating the full moon festival and thoroughly drunk. The story about Fearless being a kind of heavy draft horse is just so much fantasy. I was at my early age a competent horse woman, and when I found my way out through the back exit, I mounted one of the guard's horses and rode up north. By the time they found out that the bird had flown I was halfway up to the west bridge, and once over that, I was on Northern lands, because at that time we occupied all the land north of the river except for some small enclaves farmed by Midlanders. All the same, once over the bridge I kept going as fast as possible, past the pebble border, where I was intercepted by the Northland military who escorted me through the cleft. At first, I was confronted with disbelief, but once they were convinced of the correctness of my story I was treated with respect and admiration.

"When I say we, I mean the Northland. I call them 'we' even though I was not part of them then, but we always looked at the Midlands and the Midlanders with a level of concern, they always made us feel a bit unsafe. We were safe at the other side of the cleft, they could not touch us there, but the grounds between the river and the rocks were ours and had been cultivated by us for generations. There were some minor Midland inclusions between the pebble border and the river that belonged to individual Midlanders and were worked by them. That was accepted and caused no problems.

"We need those fertile grounds to grow the produce to feed our people. It was known at the time that a lot of Midlanders considered that the Northland territory started at the rock face and that all the ground south of the rock was rightfully theirs. Now the Midlands always maintained an active army in the form of the guards. It was an army that was well trained and too large not to be of concern to their neighbours.

"It was about three months after my escape that we had noticed a build-up of the guards. Then without warning the Midland cavalry moved in large numbers over the bridge, driving the Northlanders to the area bordering on the rock. Our forces, totally unprepared, gave little resistance. Those that fought back mostly paid for it with their lives. Even escape was difficult as the way to safety was through the cleft, one rider at a time. Of course, the invaders could not go past the cleft, as it could be defended easily. Some of our men climbed the inside of the chapel, and fired their arrows from their safe positions, causing a few casualties among the invading forces. But that was not easy as there was not much in the way of comfortable footholds.

"That is when I insisted that we had to build a walkway along the inside at a height were the men could stand and fire their arrows or throw stones, their bodies protected by the rock face. It met with a lot of objections, because the timber to build the structure had to be brought up through the gorge, an awkward task. But I insisted, got enough people interested to make a start and when the first bit was up, enough to accommodate six men and their equipment, it became clear to all the doubters that we now had a significant weapon against the Midlanders occupying the grounds adjacent to the rock.

"I now became more or less in charge of the planned counterattack. Until we had a bigger force installed, my instruction was not a significant attack, but just to harass, to make them feel unsafe, to demoralise. We always had some men up there, firing only when they had a reasonable chance of success. This way the Midlanders had to at least once a week carry a man away either dead or wounded, while not inflicting any damage on us.

"At the same time, we contaminated their water supply, which runs in part through the rock, with sewerage, so they had to get their drinking water from down the river.

"I also convinced our horsemen to set up a training program to practise drill and combat, so when we were going to attack, which all agreed we should, we would be an effective force. All available fit men started training either as cavalry or as foot soldiers.

"Soon there was an eagerness to attack, but I managed to convince them to wait till we were a hundred percent ready and then give them a forceful surprise they would never forget. We managed to do just that." She added with a wry smile, "It took us almost half a year till I was fully convinced we would beat them. By now we had a solid walkway along the inside of the rock wall in the chapel large and strong enough to accommodate fifty archers and their gear. But so far,

I had insisted not to use it as a show of strength, just for minor annoying harassment. I call it minor, but actually causing casualties on a weekly basis, so as to affect their morale.

"By now it was really me who controlled the whole operation, although I always made sure to give the impression that the army leaders, the generals so to speak, although we don't use the standard military terms, were involved and consulted, and their advice was valuable, but I always needed to convince them to use my overall strategy. I planned the day with more than one option because I wanted it to be a clear day with good views so our archers on top could do their work with the greatest effect.

"When the day came and I gave the order, the instruction for the archers on top was to clear the area adjacent to the cleft from all enemy soldiers, so our foot soldiers could emerge quickly and safely when I gave the sign. I was up there with the archers and one of the senior army leaders to oversee the action. It was the beginning of a devastating slaughter. As soon as daylight broke, and the wake-up trumpets sounded, any man within range was felled by an arrow, and in less than ten minutes complete panic raged in the Midlanders near the cleft. I now gave the sign for the foot soldiers to get out as fast as they could, both lancers and archers, and occupy and safeguard a large half circle adjacent to the cleft, so the cavalry could come out one by one without being attacked by enemy swords or lances. By now of course the Midland cavalry and foot soldiers out of reach of our archers were assembling, but being caught unawares were not ready like our forces were, who went straight into the attack extending along the rock face and overrunning most of the enemy forces.

"Here and there pockets fought back bravely but the surprise attack and the readiness of our forces and their self-assurance sowed panic among the Midlanders who saw their cavalry pushed back towards the pebble border. As there is only the one narrow path to cross the pebble border on horseback, many horsemen on reaching it dismounted, fleeing over the difficult surface on foot, while in the heat of the battle many were killed or wounded.

"It was all over in a matter of hours. I still don't know whether I would have done better by trying to pursue them further and trying to clear the whole area up to the river. But it would have been risky and difficult, and anyway we were and still are all very pleased with the result. And it has worked out all right up till recently. The devastating defeat for the Midlanders made the mood there change to 'no more war ever', which gave us a sense of security till recent events. That's why I now want a formalised border at the pebbles, so we can rest assured that Midlanders will not make a further claim on the area between the pebbles and the rock. The history is told a little different from the Midlanders point of view, yes?"

"Indeed," Marquita replied, "our story was more that the lands up to the rock belonged to us since time immemorial, and that you took the northern bit from us in a cowardly unprovoked attack. I hope that you can achieve your aims, but as you almost always manage to do that, I expect you will succeed."

17
Westland

He wiped the bloody blade on Sniffer's hide, turned and ran crying from the scene. The approaching footfalls of the horses' hooves was closing in fast. He scrambled over the pebble border, crouching low while running as fast as he could and hoped he would not be noticeable to Marculas and his men. Being on Northland territory scared him and made him feel vulnerable. The stories about the Northlanders castrating almost all men, were rife among Midlanders and made most avoid their territory. He was well aware of the fact that Marquita had not suggested he should also try to escape to the north, but instead for a later reunion on a place past the ridge they had often looked at from the swamp. It would take some time for both of them to get there.

He had planned to go straight back and pretend he had been home all the time. But Marculas and his men would recognise the remains of his horse Sniffer, and if not, then certainly by the saddle which had his name engraved on it. He had to get away as fast as he could. What would happen to him if they caught him?

But they would probably be more focussed on trying to get Marquita back, and were obviously intent to chase her on Northland territory. He was now confident that the additional obstacles he had put in their way would delay them. All the same he kept running as fast as possible, trying to keep low.

A bit further on he saw a strip of bush and small trees south of the pebble bar and as soon as he was level started to scramble back over the boulders and pebbles to the southern part where he felt safer. He briefly rested under the trees, listening carefully to see if he was being followed. He could in the clear moonlight see Marculas's men working hard to clear the path, hearing the cursing and swearing. Then he clearly heard the command: "You two see if you can find that bastard, while the rest of us hurry on." Had it taken them so little time to clear the path? "He can't be far, as he is on foot. Try the direction of the river."

"Thank you," Janitis murmured, "I stay well away from the river." He took a long drink, then started to worry, as he had not much water left in the bladder, and the river was the only source of water he could think of. The river ran just some degrees south of due west, so he worked his way in line with the pebble border which took a slightly more northern direction. Anyway, he was at least fifty to eighty metres north of the river in his estimations. He moved slowly, trying to make as little noise as possible, keeping under cover as well as he could.

A flock of birds took off noisily, protesting at being disturbed. He froze, heard the hoofbeats on the grassy slope between the river and his forest hideaway. They had noticed the obvious and come to investigate.

He crawled underneath the shrub to distance himself from where they expected him to be hiding. Just ahead was a large rocky outcrop, with dense growth behind it on a downward slope. Difficult for horses to negotiate, he must get there as quickly as he could. The riders were now so close, that he could smell the distinct horsey odour as well as hear the sound of their hooves hitting the ground. He dared not move now, while they were scanning the border between grassland and this shrub hide-away, moving slowly, just metres between them. Bit by bit they moved on, then unexpectedly came back again doing another sweep.

"Unless he managed to cross the river, he must be here somewhere, here is where there is some cover to hide."

"He could have gone north of the pebble bar."

"We can't get there in any case on horseback. Let's try once more, go into the bush as far as we can."

They were now a little distance away and going further in, making a bit of noise. *Need to get past that rock*, Janitis knew, *those horses will get too close on their next sweep when they turn*. He made use of the increased level of noise and worked himself around the rock, ignoring the racket he may make and then hurried on as quickly as he could into the dense forest beyond.

"Hey, heard him," one shouted and they cantered quickly down.

But now Janitis was quietly hiding again. *If they want to get me, they will have to get off their horses, because this is too dense for horses to penetrate. If they do that, we see who can move the fastest.* All the same his heart was now beating so loud that he felt it must be audible to them as well. Each time his pursuers were some distance away, he moved down a bit further into the centre of this dense bit of forest with solid thick undergrowth, which made it hard to move far. Then he decided to stay and keep quiet. If he kept going too far, he would walk out of the forest into open grassland. Then he would be caught. He did not know how close to the edge he was. *Better stay where I am, if they can't find me, they will get tired of it.*

He found a tree with a suitable fork about ten feet up. Climbing up there, he was well hidden because of a lower canopy below him, and dense growth all the way up. There he sat motionless, while occasionally he heard the horses move and some words of the men. Just sitting there, time did not seem to move and it was a long time before he heard a pack of horses, which were Marculas's men returning. Then his supposed captors left.

He got down noiselessly and saw that Marquita was not among the party returning from the Northland gardens. Thanks to the Almighty, she had made it. Quickly he retreated under cover again, as the guard went to the river to cross it at its shallows. He now continued through the edge of the bush, just to keep himself out of view, and aimed for the western flatlands. The edge of the forest was sudden. As if cut by a knife the forest changed into grassland. He was now a good distance away from the river, and though thirsty, kept going hoping to find some water and something edible further down. He found a shallow dip, took off his backpack and lay down, his head resting on his pack and was asleep in no time at all.

The sun was a good distance above the horizon, skirting the forest he had just left, when he awoke. He stretched, raising his head and saw in the far distance some animals grazing, unusual creatures, but as they were in a fenced off area, they must be domesticated, so probably not dangerous.

They noticed his approach, observing him intently.

What a peculiar creature, he kept thinking. Their faces were fine featured, inquisitive and appeared intelligent, reminding him of some animal he had seen somewhere before. The neck was slender merging into a quite solid body, almost horse like, but rounded. Most of the body was covered by long hair. The legs were short and rather solid.

Where there are animals, there is likely to be water, even food with a little bit of luck. His pack was in place in no time at all and it was an easy downhill walk with the sun on his back. The scenery was fresh and green, the early morning shadows long, and although thirsty and hungry, stiff and sore from all the exertions, he was invigorated by his sleep and happy that Marquita had escaped her fate. The only dampener on his feelings was the loss of his favourite horse, Sniffer. His cruel death saddened him.

The closer he came to the animals, retained in some very simple not very secure looking enclosure, the faster he moved. He jumped the fence, and one of the animals, a doe with a large swollen udder, walked up to him. Janitis started to stroke the animal, which turned its side to him. Janitis hand went for the udder, the animal did not move. He kneeled and put one of the large nipples in his mouth, sucked and felt a surge of warm milk, swallowed, sucked again and again. The doe did not move. After a while he went for the second nipple, and drank till he was full and satisfied. Hunger and thirst gone in one fell swoop.

He sighed and lay back. The bright flash of light irritating his eyes was the reflection of the keen point of a broad short blade aimed at his chest. It was firmly held by a small young fellow wearing a bright blue tunic, staring at him intently. He said something Janitis did not understand, then spoke again in a heavily accented Midland speech, staring at Janitis's attire. "Ah, so you are a Midlander and stealing our milk. Why are you here, Midlander, and if you wanted milk, why didn't you ask."

"There was no one here to ask, I was so hungry and thirsty."

"I was here."

"I did not see you, where were you then?"

The other laughed. "No, you did not see me," he said then added, somewhat roughly, "Sit up." He sat down himself, still keeping the blade pointed at Janitis's chest. "So what are you doing here, you're on western land, stealing, why?"

"I was fleeing."

"Fleeing, from who, your own people or the Northland men?"

"My own."

"You been stealing there too?"

"No, I helped the Chosen One escape. She is now in Estabella's Northland. She did not want to be chosen and be the bride of an old man, she wants to marry me," he added with pride, "so I helped her escape."

"Tell me more, the whole story." He put the sword between them.

Janitis saw his chance, grabbed the sword and pointed it at his opponent's chest, who looked at him with composed disdain. "So you took our milk, and now you are threatening to kill me? What you want now, Midlander?"

Janitis all at once felt deeply ashamed and blushed with embarrassment. He put the blade down between them, tried to say something apologetic but did not manage to get a coherent sentence out.

"What's your name, Midlander?"

"Janitis."

"I am Marmillo, now tell me your story, Janitis."

He started at first haltingly, but when he noticed Marmillo's focussed attention, he told it all in great detail, his voice wavering when he came to the bit of the mercy killing of Sniffer. His last words were when he saw the blade aimed at his chest.

"You've done well, Janitis." Marmillo offered his hand which Janitis hesitatingly shook. "You've done well, you can be proud of yourself. And what an excellent match you and Marquita will be. As you explain it, she is from a wealthy influential family and you are from a background with little possessions. In our Westland that's a perfect match. Rich must marry poor, poor must marry rich, that way things even out, and avoid accumulation of wealth."

"I wish Baruta would see it that way, even if Marquita had not been the Chosen One, he would not have allowed me to marry her, of that I am now quite sure. But we are determined, we vowed that we would be man and wife and have children. I am supposed to wait for her at a place we have seen from a distance, just over a ridge on the south side. I am sure there will be good land there to grow food, and trees to harvest to build a house from."

"That's a long way to travel, through our land first where you can get safe conduct, but it is a long way, and then you come to outlaw country, many unsavoury characters there, followed by the swamp, a dangerous place. If you get past there, the real dangers are over. Southern country is a funny place, those people are not very helpful at all, unless there is something in it for them. You can avoid the swamp area if you take the hard way through the mountain range, but then you have to cross part of the Midlands. And Marquita will have to do the same. It would be safer if you could wait for her here, then you could travel together, much safer."

"She told me where to wait and where to leave a message for her. I have no idea how she will get there, Estabella might help. I had counted on travelling back the way I came, but now that they must realise that it was me who helped her to escape, I have no idea what would happen to me if they caught me. But they would never let us unite, I just have to do as she told me and hope it all works out. I am really sure it will. So far all has gone well, including meeting you."

"You were lucky indeed. There are very few in Westland who can make themselves understood in your language. Didn't you wonder about that, being in a foreign country and being spoken to in your own tongue?"

"It did not occur to me, so why can you speak Midlandish so well, and what I did wonder about is: where were you hiding when I came here? It's very flat here and I never saw you."

Marmillo laughed. "It's called chameleon skin. A special wrap developed by our thinkers and tinkerers. It is very special, look, but don't touch, it might not like that. It just looks like a cloth, but it is alive. Whenever you wrap it around and sit or lay down, it will take on the colours and patterns from whatever it touches, see," he said and wrapping it around him he lay down on the ground and the wrap took on the colour of the ground covering, so that if you had not realised there was anything there, it is unlikely you would have noticed. Marmillo laughed. "Did you not know that Westlanders are supposed to be tall, well-built people, and here am I a very short fellow. Hardly any legs to speak of, that's why I am so short."

Janitis, feeling uncomfortable, just murmured, "Yes, you're not tall."

Marmillo laughed heartily, then noticing Janitis's discomfort, composed himself. "You would make an excellent diplomat, Janitis. But at present the Midland authorities are not likely to give you an ambassador's commission. I was first in my family to get the chameleon skin, because of my size. The raptors up there," he said, pointing at the rock edge up high, "won't attack a grown up normal sized person, but anything small, children, very small people, lambs and all very young cattle are their prey, apart from small animals likes squirrels, rabbits and the like, their preferred prey by far but not very abundant around here. That's why I have to be on the lookout for them and keep my blade always by my side and well honed, so if they grab me with their talons, I will cut their feet from their legs before they have a chance to lift me too high off the ground."

"Raptors?"

"Yes, raptors. They are an ancient beast, survived millenniums, while all the other creatures were wiped out. They survived and made their home in the rocky landscape above Westland. I would have preferred if they had been wiped out with the rest. I cannot think of any benefit they produce for our environment, but we have to be on the lookout for them all the time, a big risk for children especially.

"Well, time we go home and I introduce you to my parents, it's not every day we find an escapee on our doorsteps. I am sure they will be delighted to hear your story, but I will have to tell it for you, they don't know any Midlandish. Now we will ride, you have done enough walking for a while. You'd better take Shalina, she is already attached to you, been keeping an eye on you all the time while we were talking. I will ride her oldest son, Brot, he's small, easy to get on for me and of an easy temper, although not as placid as his mother. Come on don't dally let's get going."

"What do you call these creatures," Janitis asked, "I never seen anything like it."

"From what you told me, I understand you never been away from the Midlands. So there are many things you would not have seen, or don't know about. These are an old breed, we keep them for milk, you already know how excellent it tastes, and we clip the fur once a year, to spin and weave into a soft fabric."

"And what about the meat," Janitis asked.

Marmillo looked at Janitis disdainfully.

"Yakapaccas are family," he said. "You don't eat your family."

Riding side by side Marmillo explained about a family of Midlanders living on the foothills half a day's riding inland from the Grootes' family home. Marmillo had befriended them years ago, shortly after their arrival from the Midlands. While Marmillo had shown them the way things worked in the Westlands, the Pandilo family had taught him Midlandish, as well as how things were done where they came from. Now he was a close friend with all of the family. For a while they had been living in a small cottage close to Marmillo's home, then they acquired some medium sized holding in the foothills where they had been farming successfully ever since.

It turned out that Marmillo's family went by the name Groote, meaning big in Westlandish, which had caused some sniggers on Marmillo's part. Fortunately, he had the happy disposition that he could laugh with the laughers.

The family, after the first puzzlement about the arrival of a Midlander in their midst, followed Marmillo's explanation with obvious interest and accepted Janitis wholeheartedly in their house, so that after a few days he felt part of the family and when he raised the need for him to journey on, they raised many most valid objections. They were for the most a very happy family, only at the present time tempered by the sudden sickness of Wobbles, the toddler of the family, who had come down with symptoms indicative of poisoning by the triangular leaf herb which was growing liberally in the neighbourhood and for which no effective treatment was known.

Janitis noticing their concern, asked Marmillo to explain. "Show me the herb," he asked Marmillo. Looking around they soon found a small patch. Janitis picked a few leaves, and with Marmillo showing great concern, smelled it, bit on it then spat it out. Looking around he soon found another herb, known to him by the name 'the slender cure', smelled that, bit a piece off, chewed it and nodded. He picked a handful of it. "This is the cure for Wobbles's disease," he said.

"How do you know?"

"It grows in the lands between my home and the swamp, and the cure for the poison seems always to grow nearby. Marquita read up about it in our library. About three even sized leaves a day and in seven days he should start to improve.

Now he certainly was not allowed to leave till Wobbles improved, which happened as predicted on the seventh day.

Not all had approved of Janitis's treatment. "How should he know?" was Warda, Marmillo's younger sister's verdict. "For all we know his treatment might kill Wobbles." She had been the only one who right from the start had been not accepting of Janitis's presence and expressed disbelief in his account of what had happened. Although she had been unable to make the rest of the family doubt Janitis's story, her disbelief in his ability to cure Wobbles with the slender herb had still caused a level of uncertainty.

On day seven Wobbles, as if by magic, took more interest in his environment than he had done for more than nine days and became soon lively and communicative. Now Janitis certainly was the hero of the family, but got no praise from Warda, just sullen silence. His plans to continue his travels soon received support from Warda only, the rest of the family saying there was no hurry, stating all the possible dangers on his way down, talking at length how to combat the obstacles and threats that would be facing him. They had to accept his need to go to the agreed rendezvous with Marquita, but all knew better than Janitis did, the dangers facing him as soon as he left Westland and before reaching the Southland country which did not sound like a friendly environment; far too mercenary, but not physically full of hazards, like the Badlands, just south of the Westlands and then the pestilent swamps. The only alternative was to take the mountain road, steep and windy and a long way around, which would also involve travelling through part of the Midlands which would be dangerous for Janitis. If he was recognised the outcome was completely uncertain.

Time to go, Janitis decided at last with mixed feelings. But he had no choice, the inner compulsion was far too strong, impossible to resist. He had to start the journey that he was sure would sooner or later reunite him with his beloved Marquita.

They were all assembled on the front porch, a little awkward, as if being engaged in doing something they did not want to do. Shalina and Brot were in the paddock close by, Brot busily grazing, while Shalina seemed to be keeping an eye out towards the porch. Now all were quiet and uncomfortable, all except Warda, who was yelling out, "No, no way, he can't have her. No way she is mine. He cannot ride her, he cannot. She is my mount, she loves me the way I love her." And before anyone acted, she was off, as fast as her legs would carry her, running to the paddock on to Shalina. As Warda came alongside her, trying to mount her, Shalina stepped sideways. Warda moved close again, Shalina moved just as much away. "Come on, Shalina," Warda whispered, "I want a ride," and tried to mount her, but Shalina uncooperatively moved away. Warda got angry and tried to grab her, but now Shalina shook her off and walked a distance away.

The rest of the family on the porch followed the goings on with amusement.

"I hope you have more luck, Janitis," Marmillo's father said.

"I'm sure he will," Marmillo offered, "that one really likes him. Now let's go."

"Put this in your saddle bag, unwrap it tonight, Marmillo will tell you how to use it. Now have a good journey."

"Thank you, Master," Janitis replied, "thank you, your wife and family for your hospitality, you taught me much, and I will be forever grateful." Marmillo was busy acting as an interpreter, but even in the two weeks, Janitis had got some basic understanding of their speech, which was not as different from Midlandish as it appeared at first.

"You done us a great favour by showing us the healing powers of slender weed. Wobbles is now his old self again."

Warda moved up to the veranda, looking daggers at Janitis, and even though her mother tried, she could not be consoled. Marmillo and Janitis walked to the paddock. Shalina eagerly approached Janitis, offering her side so he could mount her with ease. The contrast was so obvious that all had trouble not to burst out laughing but they held back so as not to aggravate Warda even more. They waved and were off, at a canter first, but as soon as they were out of sight, they slowed down to an easy walking pace. Rolling grassland dotted with trees, no obviously trodden path. But Marmillo seemed to know his way about and never wavered in deciding where to go. When Janitis remarked on this he laughed.

"I know this landscape, travelled here often, and anyway there are clues such as the direction of the light at the time of the day. I'm sure you knew your way about in your part of the Midlands."

Janitis nodded, it brought his thoughts back to the foraging he and Marquita used to do. Marquita, when would they meet again?

"You're very thoughtful," Marmillo said, observing his friend.

"Just was thinking of Marquita and times past," Janitis replied, then shook it off, looked around with a happier mien, and made a comment about the beauty of their environment, which set Marmillo off on a detailed explanation about the ecology of this part of the Westlands and the crops and animals it supported.

They stopped off for lunch. Marmillo's mum had made sure they left well stocked with food for the journey. Then they set off again and travelled for a while in comfortable silence. Now and again, they resumed talking and so it went on, day after day. Marmillo explaining about the Westlands, their system of governing, which seemed very strange to Janitis.

The Westland governing body was elected by popular vote. Anyone over the age of twelve was allowed to cast a vote, and although not compelled almost all did. But to be on the list of electable candidates one had to form a body of support, which meant as many signed up supporters as possible. These lists were then submitted to an electoral selector. This was a body of twelve people who oversaw the whole process. The top twenty became the list of candidates which was distributed well before an election was due. Voters then marked their preferred choices numerically, choosing as many or few as they wished, and lodged this on election day at their nearest electoral office. This all was a very happy and enjoyable affair, with a very festive atmosphere, voters dropping off the completed forms for others. No cheating was ever heard of. This was all so much fun.

"Who did you put first," was quite a common question, with answers like, "Oh did you? He is only number nine on my list, ah well, we see who will have to do the hard work in the next eight years."

Janitis could not believe what he heard. In the Midlands it was the upper crust who chose, selected and decided; the ordinary folks had no say in it at all, mostly people born in wealth and influence had their say. With very few exceptions such as Baruta, who was from very ordinary birth, but had succeeded in climbing the ladder.

"Your electoral system, how does that work then?" Janitis asked. "With all those ones two and threes. How do they work out who is included in the end?"

"Oh, not too hard, any candidate not given a preference on the election sheet automatically gets a twenty inserted. The numbers are totalled as the forms come in and the ten lowest totals become the government for the next eight years. the person with the lowest total becomes the IC, in charge, that means. It is the only paid position as it is full time. The rest govern on a part time basis. Works well for us.

"If someone dies or is unable to carry out the job for any reason, then the next one down the list automatically fills the void, simple."

"You have ten governors, we have six elders and then the Upper Host," Janitis replied, "and of course the people's council, Baruta is one of them, if he still is. They are appointed by the householders, the men who own land."

"I like our system better," observed Marmillo, "fairer, everybody has a say. And we also have the possibility of more input. If issues develop, we organise local meetings and then give recommendations to government."

"And who appoints your guard, does the government do that?"

"Guard? Oh yes, I see what you mean, we all are the guard, every man and woman can arrest someone and bring them to the notice of the judges. Mid-term we have elections for judges. You cannot nominate yourself, you have to be nominated, and have at least twenty supporters on your list. People to be nominated must be at least twenty-five years old. When the list is put to the vote, the voting is limited to those that have successfully completed their school requirement, so as a rule are sixteen years old. And as I said we are all on guard duty all the time, but we have very little crime here, and if serious crime is proven, then the offender is forced to repay in labour or is banned to the Badlands. Anybody trying to come back from the Badlands is free for all, they can be killed without punishment. We hate killing, but Badlanders are a free for all once they enter our land."

"But the guards, how does it work?"

"When I found you taking our milk, I could have got some others and arrested you, taken you to the judges, who would have asked an explanation from you. You would have said to them what you told me, that you were desperately hungry and thirsty and did not see anyone to ask, and then the judges would have acquitted you and you would have been free to go."

So they travelled on, telling each other about their countries. It was very quiet that first day, they only met a few workers in the fields, who greeted Marmillo with enthusiasm, him responding similarly and stopping off briefly for a short talk, about the crops, the weather, their destinations, the wellbeing of their families and anything else that came to mind. They all were pleasantly amazed to meet a Midlander.

When the sun was low in the sky and the shadows lengthening, Marmillo found a nice spot sheltered from the prevailing winds. They set up a fly sheet to sleep under and lit a fire for comfort at night, to warm their food and as a deterrent from the Raptors.

"Better get your going away pressy out of your saddle bag, so I can tell you all about it, Janitis."

"Oh yes," Janitis said, "how thoughtless of me, with this all being so pleasant and exciting, forgot all about it."

Marmillo smiled. "Well, you won't forget about it quickly again."

Janitis went and fetched the parcel and started to unwrap it. It was wrapped in a thin strong material which when Janitis held it up turned out to be the Westlands flag.

"That will make you think of us," Marmillo remarked. The contents were also a material. It felt warm and strange, Janitis looked puzzled.

"Treat it with utmost care, it wants to be loved," grinned Marmillo.

"It's a chameleon skin," Janitis murmured with admiration, "a chameleon skin, my God, such a valuable present."

"Better put it under your shirt now, it likes to be close to you. It is alive, as I told you, and the better it knows you, the better it will work for you. It would not have been too happy in that saddlebag but Dad would not want you to know what it was till you were some distance away."

"How can I ever thank you and your family enough for a present like that?"

"How can we thank you ever enough for healing Wobbles? This can be very useful to you in crossing the Badlands. If you can hide from those guys, it may save you a lot of discomfort."

"So that's what he thought of, when he decided to give this to me." Janitis shook his head, tears welling up in his eyes. "You people been so good to me."

The fire was still smouldering when they woke up early the next morning. They heated a brew of herbs and yakapacca milk then set off on the next bit of the journey, and so it went day after day.

As they went on it became more and more common to meet people, Janitis being amazed at how many people, now a fair way from home, seemed to know Marmillo. He got addressed as Marmillo by some, as senor Acapillo by others, this sounded formal and respectful, and 'Hi, Shorty' by others, this often yelled with great affection, often accompanied with back slapping, laughing and a lot of happiness on both sides.

"How many people do you know and know you?" wondered Janitis.

"A fair few," was the reply. "We are a small country. We will soon pass close to East-West, the capital and largest population centre, so we will see more people on our travel but not so many will know me. Although some may still know of me, not too many people of my stature about," he laughed. And so it happened.

They skirted past the city at quite a distance, but all the same they were now travelling on more defined paths and encountered more and more people. The greetings becoming briefer, mostly just a polite nod. Marmillo showed all the signs of a man enjoying himself. But when well past and clear of East-West, he became quiet and thoughtful.

"We are now one day's travel from the Badlands, Janitis," he said. "From here on we are pretty safe as far as the raptors are concerned, they do not usually venture that far away from their rocky lairs. But as soon as you are in the Badlands new danger will threaten, as you know. I cannot come with you past the border, which is now only hours away. We will have our last camp well inside Westland, then early in the morning I will come as far as the border and then you are on your own. My only consolation is that you have the chameleon skin, it is from now your best friend."

The land sloped down at a steady pace, and soon they were in sight of the Badlands, which even from this distance looked messy and uncared for. They pitched their fly sheet and silently they got a small fire going and prepared their meals. They went to sleep early and were awake before the sun lifted above the horizon. They had their last breakfast together.

"From here you will have to go on foot, my friend," Marmillo said with a very serious expression, Shalina would not be safe, neither in the Badlands nor in the wetlands.

"I know. I have been thinking during the night. I will take the mountain path, long and arduous, but with a better chance to be safe than in the Badlands and Wetlands, I think. Shalina can't do that either. Warda will be pleased of that. But I will miss Shalina, she's been so helpful to me."

"She will never be Warda's mount, I'm sure. Warda will have to look somewhere else. But a wise decision, I think. It will take you longer to your destination. And as far as Shalina is concerned, I may very well bring her, when I come to see you when you've got yourself established a bit. I can travel quite easily across the Midland flatlands. I know where to look for you, but to help a bit keep the Westland flag flying high in the air when you have your plot established. I will not be there this or next year, but soon thereafter I hope."

"I will take the first possible turn off into the flat country. My chameleon skin can be of great help to keep me hidden if there are people about. Getting over the saddle will be the most difficult, it is very cold up there, snow and ice."

Farewell was brief; they hugged, then each went their way, Janitis slinging on his backpack and starting to climb the steep uphill path. Marmillo turned, mounted and led Shalina, who would have attempted to follow Janitis back home.

18
Years later

Janitis was resting in his cane chair, feet on an upturned crate, looking thoughtfully into the distance. His thoughts were way into the past, and from where he was now, he felt happy with his success.

But all the same the journey across the mountains that separated the southern Westlands from the Midlands had been hard and exhausting. He did not like the cold, and on top of the saddle he had to walk over ice and wade through snow. He was not well equipped for that, so had, as planned, taken the first opportunity to turn off in the direction of the flatlands. The descent was slow over snow covered stretches. From rises in the landscape he had observed the flatlands below; when there, he would have to keep himself hidden during the day and travel by night. He had been careful with his food supply but not been able to find many edible plants on his crossing.

Slugging on, eventually the snow became less deep. Each time he approached a rise or a ridge he was full of expectation what he would see from the top of the elevation. In part it now looked like a path trodden before. He stepped onto a ledge and to his amazement saw between himself and the flatlands below an isolated shelf of large proportion, dotted with primitive dwellings and some activity in the form of fires, and hairy creatures walking about. This was new and unexpected; he had never before heard that something like that existed. Then from behind a rock had stepped just such a creature, standing metres away from him, carrying a heavy club and looking at him with a mixture of contempt and suspicion. It had not been wearing clothes on top and some kind of baggy shorts below, the calves also covered in dense hair.

"Who are you?" it growled in some very heavy accented Midlandish, which Janitis was able to understand. "You are from below, what are you doing here?"

"Going home," Janitis answered flatly.

The creature pulled a face, then repeated louder, "Why are you here?"

"Coming from Westland, now going home."

"Why Westland?"

"Visit friend."

The creature looked at him searchingly. "Liar. Midlanders no friends from Westland. What are you doing here, spying on us?" Then he put two fingers in his mouth, whistling sharply and penetratingly. Two similar looking fellows came running up at full speed. His interrogator just pointed with a movement of his head at Janitis. "Take him, liar." The two had picked up

Janitis as if he was a mere feather and ran off with him downhill to their village centre.

There was a row of cages, some with livestock of some sort in them, some empty. Janitis was unceremoniously thrown in one of the empty cages. In no time at all he was being looked at by an assortment of the local population, both male and female, young and old. Some of the children threw pebbles at him, trying to cause a reaction. Most just looked silently, others were discussing him.

Now in comfort, relaxing on his terrace, he remembered the fear he had experienced, not knowing what was going to happen to him, what were they going to do to him. The fact that he was imprisoned in a livestock cage had been of great concern, were these creatures, cannibals?

He never knew how long he'd been there, but after what seemed like hours they came and took him to the square in the centre where a very old looking man was sitting on a dais with a heavy looking red cloak over his shoulders. Next to him a thin small fellow brandished a pointed stick which he dipped in a bowl with brown liquid, making marks on a sheet of papery material. It was he who asked the same questions Janitis had been asked before.

This time Janitis told him that he was only passing through his home country briefly to get as quickly as possible to south country to try and find work to get some money to buy food. The question about spying came up again and again, this obviously being their main concern. Then he was returned to his cage, which now had some straw in it, a bowl of water and some fruit. He had to find a means of escaping, as soon as possible. That thought fuelled by fear had been foremost in his mind. And the way it had worked out still filled him with satisfaction.

The night was closing in. Apart from some light coming from the primitive huts, there was a flare in the central square, but all was pretty quiet. A guard, armed with a heavy club and a dagger in his belt, did the rounds, peering in at the cages now and again, wandering slowly around. Janitis noticed him peering in and looking at him before wandering on. Next time around Janitis flattened the straw, spread it around to make sure the guard would not assume him being asleep under there, then went and flattened himself close to the gate as much as he could and pulled the chameleon skin over himself, peering from underneath as soon as he heard the guard come near.

The guard had stopped now, looking in, peering intently, trying to see Janitis, but could not discern anything in the cage at all. If he would then go and get help, Janitis would make himself visible while he was not being watched. But the guard kept peering for what seemed forever, then Janitis had heard the noise of the slide bolt moving and the chain clanging against the metal frame. The guard was going to have a closer look. Janitis, every muscle tense, hoped he would step inside, which he did, with utmost care, slowly going in step by step, prodding with his club. He was just about a stride inside when Janitis saw his opportunity, slid through the open gate, closed it, put the slide bolt in place and made a run for the far end of the village, while he now heard the loud screams of the guard.

He soon jumped the perimeter fence at the far end, and kept going. But once out of the light of the flare he had to pick his way with care, as the night offered little visibility. Now he could hear a lot of commotion from the village. Looking back, there were now a number of flares around, and the area being searched in ever wider circles.

Anyway, he had been able to escape them and got down to the Midlands, where of course he had to avoid detection, travelling at night and keeping hidden as well as he could during the days. He survived by stealing fruit and veggies eaten raw from the farms, and it had been such a relief when he eventually entered Southland. Fortunately, he arrived there at fruit picking time, thin and exhausted, but in good spirits, and from there on it had all been uphill. He had been able to provide for himself, sleep rough for a very long time, but when the Southerners knew he was a good worker, he never was without work, able to save money and start building his house on free land away from the centre.

No one else had done such a thing before, it drew the attention. He grew some fruit and veggies near his abode. He had been right in assuming that over the hill there would be fertile soil, and it was not long before he was a regular presence at the weekly markets.

So far all was good, he was respected, accepted as an unusual part of the community. He had been encouraged by more than one girl for getting involved. But by now it was common knowledge that he was waiting for someone to arrive as soon as she could. Some started to feel sorry for him, thinking he was obsessed by some kind of silly dream. But even though all was fine, he quite often felt terrible lonely. He had three friends, Marmillo in Westland, Breer in his home place, not too far away but out of reach, and his love, Marquita, now in Northland. The Southlanders were friendly, but he had no friends here that he could be comfortable with.

He closed his eyes for a moment, and when opening them again realised he had been asleep for a while as the sun had sunk low in the sky and it was getting dark. In the far distance he saw some movements which he could not quite place, foreign to him. It was hard to work out what was going on there from this distance with the light as dim as it was now. But one thing was soon sure, he could see fires being lit and the presence of horses. *Well, better go to sleep, all will be clearer in the morning light.*

Getting up and stretching early morning, he had a quick look at what was happening at the western end of the village. Now clearly there were fires going, men and what looked like tiny horses were moving about but hard to work out from this distance. First breakfast, then a few hours work in the veggie garden, then a break for some morning tea. Sitting on the veranda, he watched a line moving his side of the centre like an elegant pencil line on a piece of paper, the line slowly moving right to left in front of him, past where he sat then turning in an upwards direction towards him, then starting to move left to right, the sort of path he took when he came home on his horse.

Now he could see more clearly, it was a train of horses, tiny ones at that, two abreast, he started to count. Two rows of two horses up front, then one on its own, a bay horse slightly bigger than the rest, then followed by three more rows of two, and heading up this way. He got a little concerned, what should any party that big want of him? The row going ever so slowly, they did not seem in any hurry, passing for the second time left to right, now all clearly visible.

He now focussed on the single rider, bay horse, rider dressed differently. *Ah, a woman, ah, no, not possible, not possible yes, must be, yes, it is, Marquita. She found me, she came, why the retinue, never mind, it is her, she is here.* Janitis did not bother to mount his horse but started running straight down as fast as his legs would take him, Marquita, the one he had been waiting for, for so long.

Marquita stopped her horse, dismounted and also

began to run, uphill for her. When they were close, they both stopped in their tracks and looked at each other, then two more steps and they were in each other's arms.

19
Reunion

Janitis sat on the veranda looking over the downwards slope towards the centre, then slowly scanned his environment up to the horizon, then the sky. He sighed with satisfaction. Inside, Marquita was breastfeeding his two sons. She had borne him twins last week, two healthy boys. The delivery had been an easy one, and Marquita herself radiated good health and satisfaction. He was a happy man, he was a very happy man. It had taken awhile for Marquita to come and find him, but it had given him time to establish a productive market garden and build a house. Although basic it serviced their needs, and after the arrival of Marquita all had proceeded at much more than twice the speed.

What a girl she was, what a woman she had proven to be. It had taken three years for her to come and find him. Not once had he asked why it took her that long, he had just scooped her up in his arms, and that very day they were formally married by a qualified official among her entourage. Since then, all had been bliss.

The three years before her arrival had been busy ones. It was his busy work schedule that kept loneliness at bay. He had to pick fruit and do labouring work to earn enough to buy a horse, building materials for his house and seed and plants to start his market garden. As a worker he was in demand. 'That skinny Midlander works like a horse you know, and he has good sense as well.' He had no time for leisure, but it did not matter, because he was never invited to any of their gatherings or parties. They respected him for what he was, but he always remained that Midlander up the hill. In those three years he had made no friends, nobody that he could spend an evening nattering with just over a drink, none had invited him for a meal in their house. They almost without exception were polite and friendly and mostly scrupulously honest.

Twice, different good looking young women had shown an interest in him, seeing good value and prospects in the young, good-looking, hard-working fellow. But he had not encouraged them. After a while it was common knowledge that he was awaiting the arrival of a mystery woman to share his life and future with. There had been some shoulder shrugging and sniggers about that, when after months the woman did not materialise. There were some expressions like, "Poor Janitis. Nice but a little strange, ah well."

And then one afternoon, along their northern border, this cavalcade had arrived, travelling carefully and with circumspection, always making sure they were not invading anybody's private territory. Eleven riders in all, one a woman riding the largest of the horses, but even so, that one was small too. They had camped overnight at the bottom of the rise, well out of the centre and early the next morning wound their way up to Janitis's residence. The mystery woman had arrived.

It caused enormous speculation and gossip. Four of the riders had come to town, to trade for supplies, paying well in rare metal and delicate handmade ornaments; always their actions made it clear that they were on foreign territory. The Southerners knew a good deal when they saw one and tried to extract maximum benefit from these meetings. There had been a very quiet party up the hill. Two days later the cavalcade returned the way they had arrived leaving the woman behind.

Janitis was happy, Janitis was satisfied. He scanned his environment knowing that all had turned out for the best.

A lone rider emerged from a heavily timbered area to his right. The rider seemed from this distance very old, but Janitis noticed immediately that he was one with his mount, an experienced rider. He approached a single tree on the edge of a garden bed, then dismounted. Janitis had a sharp intake of breath, jumped up and started running towards the old man, yelling, "Dad… Dad," then embracing him, tears streaming down his face. His dad, Jacquito, not used to such an emotional display, returned the embrace awkwardly.

"How did you get here. Past the swamps and all that?"

Jacquito turned around, pointing at the bush border. "Your friends took me."

"My friends?"

"Breer and the one with the short legs, I keep forgetting his name."

Two riders emerged from the bush and approached abreast. One of the two yakapaccas trailing Marmillo surged ahead, nose held high sniffing the air and went straight for Janitis and began muzzling his face.

"Shalina." Janitis put his hand around the animal's neck. "You lovely beast." Then he ran forward to Marmillo and Breer who had dismounted, embracing one after the other and then again. "By God, what a day what a day this is."

He was so overcome by emotion that he did not know what to do or to say. "Marquita, Marquita."

"Yes, what's up?" Marquita, finishing putting the twins in their cot, stepped outside, straight into her brother's arms.

"Breer, what a surprise. It's been so long, so good to see you. And Marmillo and Jacquito. I can't believe it, all of you here." She hugged both then Breer again. "This is unbelievable, I can't believe my eyes. Oh, Janitis, show your dad his grandsons. He'll be so proud."

Bottles of wine and juice were brought out, food put on the table outside, all gave a hand. Stories had to be told, each had their own tale to tell.

"Jacquito, Pop, how did this happen?"

"Well," Jacquito started hesitantly, "this fellow here," pointing at Marmillo, by now he had again forgotten that funny name he couldn't get his head around for some reason or another. "This fellow rode up trailing these funny furry animals and asked me if I knew someone by the name of Breer.

"'Why do you want to know that?' I asked. 'Well,' he said, 'I want to take him to his friend and brother-in-law Janitis.' I said, 'Say that again, to whom?'

"'Janitis, he's a friend of mine too.' By now I was thoroughly confused. 'Where do you know this Janitis from?'

"'Well, he passed by our house in the Westland. He comes from here somewhere, and I expect to find him somewhere on the other side of that mountain range.' I was quite taken aback.

"'Is he a young fellow?'

"'About sixteen years old, I think.'

"'Then he's my son, no other Janitis of that age lives here.'

"'Your son, then you know where he lives.'

"'No, I don't, I have never been even anywhere near that mountain, there's the swamp in between and we all stay well away from the swamp.' Anyway, that's the way it came all about. We all got here past the swamp, nothing dangerous happened. "We lived so close by all that time and I never knew."

Then it was time for Marquita to tell the story of her escape from Super Castle. Only Janitis had heard it before but did not mind hearing it all again. Her experiences at Northland could wait for another time, but all wanted to hear how she managed to get away. She told it in great detail. How she deceived Ariotto, naive simple minded Ariotto. This embarrassed her greatly, but everybody else thought it funny enough to frequently burst out in laughter. They all were tense during the retelling of how she was chased and almost caught, till she came to the part where she could hear her pursuer only a horse length away, then the sound like the crack of a whip and a terrible crash. She had never been able to work out what happened.

"It was not me," Janitis interposed. "I was sitting under the bridge getting terribly worried hearing that she was being pursued, but unable to do anything. I too heard a sound like the crack of a whip, then a frightful crash, but Fearless' hooves still pounded the ground. It's a mystery we have not been able to solve or understand."

Breer looked sheepishly uncomfortable.

"What's the matter with you, Breer?" Marmillo smiled, getting a feeling of what might have happened. "Do you reckon it was the cracking of a whip, they heard?"

"Of course it was," Breer replied.

"How can you be so sure?"

"Because it was my whip."

"What?" Janitis and Marquita stood up as one, but it was Marquita who had her arms around her brother's neck first. "It was you, you saved me. You took an incredible risk. If you had been found out, your life would not have been worth living. Dad would have killed you and buried you in your veggie patch."

Breer laughed. "He would not have gone that far, but I would have been very unpopular for a long time. I had to do something. I was going to trip up Swift with a rope, but there was no time to fix that, he was so close behind you. So all I could do was crack the whip on his nose and that had disastrous results for a beautiful horse and some discomfort for its rider, but you got away, that's all that matters."

They celebrated and enjoyed each other's company for days on end. The twins were admired. When all were about, Janitis announced the naming.

"Don't I have a say in this?" Marquita enquired.

"I don't expect you will disagree with my choices. Marmillo Jacquito for the smaller of the two, Breer Jacquito for the other fellow. Happy with that?"

"Very happy."

Janitis received many compliments about his market garden and the house he had built. "But now it is time for me to give some attention to my garden, so I will leave early tomorrow morning. I can easily do it in one day," Breer announced.

"I'd better come with you," Jacquito said. "I'm not keen to go past the swamp on my own and what's his name here, having come all that way from Westland, will be staying a bit longer, I'm sure."

"Why don't you stay a bit longer too, Pop?" Marquita said. "We haven't seen you for so long and you can enjoy Janitis's and your grandsons' company."

"And yours," he added, shyly. "But I have to go back to look after the animals."

"I'll do that for you," Breer volunteered.

"You can stay as long as you like," Marquita said. "As a matter of fact, you can stay forever," she added. "We can do with another pair of hands."

"They are slow old hands now, and I still got a belly to fill."

"Oh, come off it, Dad, you can teach the kids to ride horses when they are grown a bit, and what are the good and the bad herbs."

Jacquito seemed to hesitate for a moment. "Yes, I could do that. It's been rather lonesome by myself since you left, Janitis. Okay, I'll do that."

"And I might hang on a bit longer, if I may," Marmillo added.

"You are welcome to stay as long as you like, Marmillo."

"Now that you know how easy and close by it is, you can visit me too, Janitis," Breer said.

"No, I will never go to the Midlands again," declared Janitis.

"It's safe now for you to do so, I'm sure. Marquita is quite popular now, particularly among the young. Many now wear rosettes with your name on it, sis, and one of our leading horticulturists has come up with a new flower he calls a Marquita. If you visit us, you could fill halls with talks about your experience, you're a bit of a cult figure now. And then you could highlight Janitis's part in your escape. Not so much is known about his part at all, mainly assumptions. You know of course, or maybe you don't, that our new Upper has issued an edict renouncing his right to marry the Chosen One. It is more or less expected to be followed by a new edict disbanding the habit all together. There still will be a Chosen One and the usual festivities, but now she will be allowed to marry anyone, in line with the established customs. Not enough for some of the younger ones, who call themselves Marquitas, who want to stop the parents' choosing of the partner and leave the choice completely to the girls themselves, but I cannot see that happening soon."

"And what about you, Breer, when are you going to marry?"

"I'm married to my veggie and flower beds and that will do me fine. But come and visit me."

"I'm happy here," was Janitis's immediate reply. "I have everything I want. I have no desire ever to go to the Midlands."

Marquita raised her eyebrows, smiling at Breer, signalling an uncertain reply. His telling of her popularity back home certainly amazed her. But for now, all her commitments were to Janitis and the twins.